Truelove Hills

Mystery at Pebble Cove

PATRINA McKENNA

Copyright © 2019 Patrina McKenna

All rights reserved

This book is a work of fiction. Names, characters, places, and incidents either are products of the author's imagination or are used fictitiously. Any resemblance to actual persons, living or dead, events, or locales is entirely coincidental.

Publisher: Patrina McKenna

patrina.mckenna@outlook.com

ISBN-13: 978-0-9932624-6-3

Also by Patrina McKenna

The **GIANT Gemstones** *series*

Feel good fantasy for the whole family!

GIANT Gemstones
A Galaxy of Gemstones
The Gemstone Dynasty
Enrico's Journey
Summer Camp at Tadgers Blaney Manor

The **Truelove Hills** *series*

Romantic comedy with a twist!

Truelove Hills
Truelove Hills – Mystery at Pebble Cove
Truelove Hills – The Matchmaker

DEDICATION

For my family and friends

PROLOGUE

5 November 1920

The boat rocked from the weight of the stones, nine bags of them. It was just before dawn when Josiah Tomlin reached the private beach that led to his home. He had no time to spare – he had to get the bags inside before daylight. There was a door in the side of the cliff at Pebble Cove that led to the basement of Josiah's house, and he hauled the bags inside. He could carry two at a time, and he was on the third trip when he fell onto the beach with a searing pain in his back.

Josiah daren't move. He'd been shot, and he watched in silence as the assailant retrieved the bags of stones and hauled them into another boat moored out of sight of the cove. Josiah recognised his attacker straight away and he kept still while he hatched a plan. Dawn was breaking when she pulled the final bag past his rigid body, and he grabbed her drenched cloak. Her ear-piercing scream scattered the gulls. 'Please help me. I stole your husband's emeralds so that I could help you escape from him. I've heard how he beats you. No woman should have to suffer at the hands of a man.'

Mary Finchinglake removed the large hood that covered most of her face, and her light brown hair fell in waves over her shoulders. How could she believe any bad of Josiah Tomlin? He'd worked for her husband for many years. Mary fell to her knees in exhaustion. A shudder encompassed her as she looked up at the house on the cliff and the grounds beyond it that led to the chateau. Her heart pounded, daylight was looming, and she had to think quick.

Josiah leant on Mary's shoulders as they trudged through the water to her boat. He was impressed with his idea and he hoped Mary would fall for it. 'My blood is on the beach, and the boat I stole from your husband is moored there. This could be your escape from him, Mary. You need to hide me and the emeralds until he's locked away. With any luck, he'll be hanged, that will be justice for what he's done to you.'

It took every ounce of energy for Mary to row the heavily-laden boat away from Pebble Cove. She didn't know whether to be annoyed with Josiah Tomlin, or grateful. She'd been planning to escape with the emeralds from her dowry since her husband had knocked her to the floor in his last drunken rage. Mary was a woman of means, with a will to go with it. James Finchinglake preferred people to believe he was dealing in contraband rather than living off his wife and he was keen to flash the emeralds around. He was vile and repulsive, and Mary should never have married him.

*

James Finchinglake was sent to the gallows for the "murder" at Pebble Cove, and Mary nursed Josiah back to health until it was safe for him to escape to America to begin his new life with a bounty of emeralds in a large leather purse. Josiah couldn't believe his luck. He'd never intended helping Mary. He'd stolen the emeralds so that he could leave his wife who was having an affair with the Lord at the chateau.

It was almost a perfect plan, except for the low flying aircraft that was surveying the coastline when Mary and Josiah made their exit from Pebble Cove in the clear light of day on 5 November 1920. Josiah had heard that aerial photographs were the latest thing and an exhibition was being held the following summer in London: "England's Coastline from the Air." Josiah prayed that the aircraft hadn't been taking images on the morning of his "murder". Still, once he was in America, it would be Mary's problem not his – Josiah's new life was just beginning.

1

HANNAH'S HOUSE

One Hundred Years Later

Spring had arrived in Truelove Hills, and daffodils lined the long private drive from the main road to Hannah's house; daffodils in pots. Once the contracts had been signed to buy the property from Lady Leticia Lovett six months ago, Hannah had been on a mission to complete the renovation work by spring. With the invasion during the winter months of diggers, lorries and tipper trucks, there wasn't much Hannah could do in the garden of a house on the side of a cliff, but she could plant bulbs in pots and place them where she wanted when it was time for her to move into her new home with Arthur Junior. Finally, that day had come, and Hannah, AJ and the Makepeace family stood in the glossy white kitchen of the once derelict building.

David Makepeace poured the prosecco. 'It's a bit

early for this, but let's have a toast to Hannah. The way my daughter has managed this building project has been second to none. I'd never have thought this place would have been finished so soon. To Hannah!'

AJ sipped his juice through a straw, and David's three younger daughters held their glasses out for a top up. Matilda spoke on behalf of her twin sisters, Tabitha and Tallulah. 'Well, Hannah has had us all on our hands and knees scrubbing floors, painting walls and keeping the builders supplied with endless refreshments. I think we deserve a mention too.'

David laughed as he lifted the bottle. Arthur Senior patted Matilda's husband on the back. 'Don't forget about Theo. He's the one that's kept the peace with Leticia all winter with her castle's grounds being dug up. She went into a real hissy fit at one stage until Theo calmed her down with his charm.'

Matilda giggled. 'Oh, Grandpa, you do exaggerate! I think Lady Lovett was most annoyed when Fluffy kept digging up her flower beds.'

Arthur bent down to pat his little white dog. 'Fluffy was only searching for bones, weren't you boy? He's found several over the last few months. It's not his fault Leticia couldn't keep her garden secure while the building work was going on.'

Hannah raised her glass. 'Well, I'd like to thank you

all for everything you've done to help AJ and me. I could never have imagined, when we were living in our apartment in Dubai less than a year ago, that we would be here now in our own home in Truelove Hills.'

Arthur raised his glass. 'It's good to have you home, Hannah. It's good to have all of my family back where they should be.'

What a year it had been for Arthur, at one stage he didn't want to leave his pebblestone cottage. He'd lost his beloved wife, Alice, his four granddaughters had left the village, and his world was in pieces. Now the girls were all back. Matilda had a husband and Hannah a four-year-old son. The Makepeace family was growing.

Tabitha and Tallulah took hold of AJ's hands. 'Let's go down to Pebble Cove with the fishing nets Grandpa's found for us.' Tabitha opened the front door.

Arthur called out. 'Don't forget the bucket!'

When Arthur had suggested that Hannah buy the house on the edge of the grounds of Chateau Amore de Pebblio, he'd remembered the fun he'd had playing in it with his friend Billy Tomlin, over eighty years ago. There was only one way down to Pebble Cove in those days, and that was through a door in the floor of the kitchen. Arthur remembers the excitement counting all ninety-nine steps before reaching beach level.

Arthur hoped that Hannah hadn't spoiled the fun for AJ. She'd employed an army of builders to carve an easier access route down the side of the cliff. You couldn't drive to the private cove, but you could walk, and there were now shallow steps and handrails and two platforms to take a break on the way down. Hannah had placed a bench on each of the platforms, one in memory of her mother, Harriet, and another to remember her grandmother, Alice.

Hannah ushered her family into the yellow and white lounge with stunning sea views. 'Take a seat everyone. I've got some exciting news.'

Matilda chuckled. 'Don't tell me that Bob the Builder has finally asked you out?'

Hannah blushed. 'I told you before; his name's Robert, Rob Sharnbrook. Anyway, he hasn't asked me out. He's popping around in a week or so to check that there are no snagging issues with the building work, but that's about it. My news is much more significant than that.'

Theo sat forward on the sofa. With his tousled brown hair, dark brown eyes, and dimpled smile, Hannah could see why Matilda had fallen for him. 'Please tell us, Hannah, you have us in suspense.'

'Well, you all know that I put my private law firm

on hold while I've been managing the renovation work. Now that we've moved in, it's perfect timing that Lady Lovett has found me my first client!'

David Makepeace nodded in approval, but Arthur was concerned. 'Now, I've been meaning to mention this, don't go bringing any clients to your home, it's a bit remote out here. It's important you get yourself an office.'

Hannah smiled. 'Well, I've got lucky. Lady Lovett has said that I can use a room at the chateau whenever I need to meet my clients. She said that the client she's found would prefer the discretion anyway. I've got a good rapport going with Leticia; she says it's fun having another girl to talk to, and her staff make the best cappuccinos.'

Matilda's eyes widened. 'Who's the client?'

Hannah shrugged her shoulders. 'I don't know, it all sounds very hush hush. I can't wait to meet him tomorrow.'

Arthur's silver moustache twitched. 'So, it's a man then. Be careful, Hannah.'

Hannah laughed. 'Oh, Grandpa, most of my clients in Dubai were men, and I didn't get into any trouble over there did I?'

Arthur kept his silence and stood up to look out of

the window at his two granddaughters and great-grandson fishing in a rockpool below. After Harriet died when the girls were so young, Alice and Arthur had given up their retirement to raise them and by the time Alice died they were all young women. Now, Arthur felt he had to shoulder the responsibility alone. His only son was far too busy running the Solent Sea Guest House and the King Arthur public house to keep an eye on the family.

'Grandpa, you're not answering me.'

Arthur turned to face his beautiful, intelligent granddaughter with her long curly black hair and the usual Makepeace green eyes – Matilda was the only one with Harriet's blue eyes – 'I was lost in my thoughts, Hannah. I'll always worry over you girls. You know that.'

Hannah and Matilda stood either side of their grandfather and Matilda linked arms with him. 'We know you will, Grandpa, you're our knight in shining armour always making sure we're on the right path.'

Arthur rubbed his hands together and headed towards the front door. 'Race you to the beach!'

2

A NEW CLIENT

Hannah recognised him straight away when he entered her office in the chateau; Tobias Finchinglake, owner of Finchinglake Vineyard. From the pictures she'd seen in a glossy magazine, he was married with two young children and approaching forty.

'Mr Finchinglake, it's a pleasure to meet you. My name's Hannah Makepeace, and I'm happy to advise you on your legal issues.'

Tobias Finchinglake surveyed Hannah from top to toe, and she felt instantly on edge. 'How do I know I can trust you, Miss Makepeace?'

Hannah breathed in deeply and handed her potential new client a copy of her references, he read them before holding out his hand.

'You've got the job, Hannah. Call me Toby from now on and if there's any leakage of my case I will sue you.'

Hannah shook Toby's hand and a spark of electricity shot between them. That wasn't a good start. There was definite tension in the room and Toby strode to the door before opening it and peering out into the corridor. Returning to his seat opposite Hannah, he began to articulate his requirements.

'There have been discrepancies in my finances over the last two months.'

Toby held his head in his hands and leant forward onto Hannah's desk. She could see a few grey hairs amongst the mass of light brown. Toby sat up and looked Hannah straight in the eyes.

Hannah blushed and looked down at her notepad. 'Surely your accountant can identify the anomalies?'

'That's the problem. He can't. That means I don't trust him. I need you to be my eyes and ears to get to the bottom of it, and the only way you can do that is for me to employ you at the vineyard as a business consultant.'

Hannah placed her pen down on her notepad. 'I think we've got our wires crossed here, Toby. I'm a lawyer, not an accountant or private investigator, and I'm definitely not a business consultant.'

Toby stood up and paced around the room. 'Would it help if I told you my accountant's name is William Tomlin?'

Hannah shook her head, and Toby continued. 'Will's family originates from Truelove Hills.'

Hannah reached for a glass of water. 'My grandfather advised me that his friend, Billy Tomlin, used to live in my house with his mother who was the housekeeper at this chateau.'

Toby's eyes shone like pools of liquid silver. 'I just knew it. I had a feeling there was a connection between us. Will's a nice enough guy, but an accountant that can't substantiate where my money's going needs to be looked into and you're going to help me get to the bottom of it.'

Hannah opened her mouth to protest, and Toby raised a finger to his lips. 'This is just between the two of us. I don't want anyone else finding out.'

*

On her way down the pebblestone High Street from the chateau to the King Arthur, Hannah struggled to contain her excitement. There was something about this mission for Toby that intrigued her. It wasn't her usual type of work, but it paid well, and she was keen to learn more about Finchinglake Vineyard.

Hannah opened the door to the pub to the sight of Bruce and Steve Copperfield working behind the bar and Tabitha and Tallulah playing in the garden with AJ. Tallulah waved at the sight of her sister peering through the window and ran into the lounge bar to greet her. 'Matilda's waiting for us in Cindy's Bakery. She thought we could all have a catch up on your new client.'

Cindy Copperfield was an established businesswoman in the village. With the help of Theo, Head of Tourism, she owned three businesses in the lane opposite the pub. Her bakery, delicatessen and bistro were all doing well since the village had changed its name from Pebblestown to Truelove Hills last year. The funding from her husband's father, Lord Sonning-Smythe, had been a godsend in getting things off the ground. Cindy twisted her wedding ring several times a day. She could barely believe the change in things since Theo had turned up in the village just over a year ago. Now Cindy was married to Theo's friend, Jamie, and six months' pregnant.

AJ pressed his nose against the bakery door, and Cindy reached for a gingerbread man; that would keep AJ occupied while the girls had a chat. Late afternoon was the quietest time after the lunchtime rush, and with no customers to attend to, Cindy sat down with her best friend, Matilda, and Matilda's three sisters. AJ was left to roam around the shop eating his biscuit with his mother's eyes following his every move.

Tallulah was the first to speak. 'Well, Hannah, tell us all about your new client. Is he handsome? Married? What sort of trouble has he been in that he needs a lawyer?'

Hannah peered over her teacup, then placed it down and crossed her fingers under the table. Her sisters would never give up on grilling her unless she put them off track. 'He's a very old friend of Leticia's who needs me to sort out some legal issues to free up his finances. All quite boring stuff really.'

Tallulah yawned. 'I never knew why you went into that job in the first place. There's no excitement in Law. Tabitha and I have much more fun doing paintings for Matilda's shop and working with Cindy's brothers in the pub.' Tabitha raised her eyes at that last comment.

Matilda stood up. 'Well, if that's all the news, then I'd best get back to work. Theo's covering for me. Let me know when AJ needs looking after next, we're always happy to help.'

AJ climbed onto Hannah's lap and handed her the gingerbread man's remaining leg. 'Is that for me, darling? That's very kind of you.'

AJ wiped his hands over Hannah's jacket, and Tallulah sniggered. 'I told you not to go for all that white in your house. AJ will be leaving marks all over the place.'

Hannah smiled and stroked her son's dark curly hair. 'There's nothing a touch of paint won't fix or a steam cleaner – I'll need to order one. That reminds me, we must pop into the Post Office & General Store on the way home, there's a parcel for me to collect.'

*

Mrs Carruthers was delighted to see Hannah and AJ. She'd written out a New Home card to give to them when they next popped into the Post Office & General Store. 'Hannah and little AJ, what a sight for sore eyes. My day's been decidedly dull until you turned up.'

Hannah kissed Mrs Carruthers on the cheek. The poor woman hadn't been quite herself since she'd discovered her boyfriend of five months, Eric Brimstone, had a wife. Mrs Carruthers was in her seventies now, and Eric may have been her last chance of finding a partner with whom to share her life. Hannah shuddered, it could be lonely at times without someone to confide in or go out with. Still, Hannah had AJ, and he was all she needed.

'Anyway, Hannah, how are things going between you and that nice builder? Now, that was a bit of excitement earlier, he dropped by and bought a bunch of yellow roses. If he hasn't given them to you then they must be for his mother, or God forbid, his wife. I don't trust any man anymore. You must come across all sorts in your line of work. I bet you get involved with divorces and alimony and all the gossip that goes with it.'

Hannah smiled and guided AJ to the door. 'We'll see you again soon, Mrs Carruthers, thanks for the card.'

*

Hannah and AJ turned left out of the shop, it was over the road from her grandfather's cottage, the guest house and pub, and on the same side of the High Street as Matilda's Memorabilia, her sister's gift shop. They climbed the hill to Chateau Amore de Pebblio and turned left just before it to walk down the long driveway to their cliffside home.

AJ pulled one of the daffodils from a pot and handed it to his mother. Hannah scowled before forcing a smile. 'That's lovely, AJ, but please don't pick me any more flowers. They need to stay in the garden.'

AJ ran ahead, and Hannah watched as he reached the house. He stood by the front door waving his arms in the air. 'Mummy, Mummy!' Hannah caught up with him to find a bunch of yellow tulips lying on the doorstep. That was strange, Mrs Carruthers had mentioned yellow roses, not tulips. Hannah picked the flowers up and searched for a card; there wasn't one. It was too much of a coincidence for them not to have been from Rob. Hannah unlocked the door and walked into the kitchen to find a vase. That was a nice gesture. She'd have to thank him when he came around to go through the snagging list.

3

FINCHINGLAKE VINEYARD

It was Hannah's first day at work as a "business consultant", and Toby was keen for her to meet Will Tomlin. 'Will, let me introduce you to Hannah . . . Lawful, she's going to be coaching me on some business issues over the next few weeks. You'll see her around on occasions.'

Will shook Hannah's hand. 'Pleased to meet you, Hannah.'

Toby opened his office door and let Hannah walk through first. He lowered his voice. 'This isn't going to be as easy as I thought. I couldn't use your real name, or Will would have picked up on it straight away. The Makepeace's are well-known in Truelove Hills.'

Hannah suppressed a giggle. 'Well, you could have

chosen something better, it sounds like Hannah *Awful!* I was called better things by the bullies at school.'

Toby frowned. 'Were you bullied at school?'

Hannah shook her head. 'No, of course not, I just got teased because I was always top of the class. Now, let's get on with business. Where do you want me to start?'

*

After a morning scrutinising the accounts in Toby's office, Hannah was more than ready for lunch. 'Well, Toby, as you have established, your finances have dropped off over the last two months but, as I have advised, I'm not the best person to look into this. I'm a lawyer, not an accountant.'

Toby didn't falter. 'I don't care; I need you. You're the only person I can trust.'

Hannah was taken aback at Toby's persistence. Still, she had warned him of her capabilities, and he wasn't concerned, so she may as well enjoy the next few weeks while she helped him with his mission.

At the end of the day, Toby advised her when she would next be required. 'There's a charity event on Friday night in the barn over there.' Toby nodded to a large barn through the window. 'It's nothing too pretentious. I'd like you to attend to keep an eye on

Will. You may overhear some things after he's had a few, he's bringing his new girlfriend so he'll be trying to impress her. If he knows where my money's going, it's bound to come out at some stage.'

Hannah could see Toby's point. 'I'll be there. What time, and what's the dress code?'

'Seven o'clock and whatever you wear to a barn dance.'

Hannah laughed. 'It'll be good to meet your wife. She looks lovely in the photos. I guess it'll be too late for your young children to come along. I'll need to get a babysitter for my son too.'

Toby nodded. 'See you Friday night then.'

*

Friday couldn't come quick enough, Hannah was looking forward to playing private investigator, she had a notepad and pen in her bag and intended to note down any incriminating conversations she overheard during the evening.

Toby welcomed Hannah with a handshake and introduced her to Sophie. Hannah was disappointed not to be sitting on their table. She was on one at the far end of the barn positioned next to Will and Lara. As Toby had predicted, Will's tongue loosened after a few drinks and Hannah leant back towards him to hear the conversation with his girlfriend. 'That necklace looks great on you. I'll get you the bracelet next month. I need to save up a bit.'

Hannah shook her head. So that was where Toby's money was going – it was adorning Lara! All Toby had to do now was keep an eye on the accounts and check every transaction against the invoices and receipts. An internal audit was all that was needed, and Will would soon be caught out with embezzling company funds. Hannah's job was done. She felt disappointed to have solved the case so quickly.

A hand brushed Hannah's shoulder. 'As you haven't got a partner, I'll have to share myself around, will you join me for the next dance?'

Toby held out his hand, and Hannah took it. The charity barn dance was a frantic occasion, not the time for divulging secrets and discrediting the company's accountant. As would be expected, the wine was excellent, and Hannah managed to drink a few glasses between dances. It was such a treat to have an evening out. AJ was spending the night at the guest house with her father, and she'd booked a taxi for midnight.

*

The evening came to a close, and Hannah searched for Toby and Sophie to say "goodbye". She could feel Toby staring at her from across the barn, but there was no sign of Sophie. Come to think of it she hadn't seen Sophie since the beginning of the evening. She hoped they hadn't had a row. Hannah waved, and Toby rushed over.

'I just wanted to say thank you for a lovely evening and to say goodbye to your wife, but I can't see her anywhere.'

Toby lowered his eyes. 'Oh, she left early. Had to get back for the children, you know what it's like.'

Hannah tried not to slur her words. 'Well, I've found out where your money's going. That's *my* job done.'

Toby frowned. 'Let's meet up in my office in the morning. See you at nine o'clock.'

Hannah leant forward to kiss Toby on the cheek, just as he bent down to untangle his watch strap from her sleeve. They bumped heads, and he held her in his arms for a moment, his watch strap ripping the material. 'I'm so sorry, let me know the cost of a new dress. It's the least I can do.'

Hannah lowered her head to hide her blushes, she decided against the kiss. 'It's no problem. It's only an old dress anyway. I've had it for years.'

*

The following morning, Toby sat at his desk and

listened to Hannah's revelations. 'So, you see, Toby, Will is somehow syphoning off your money to pay for his girlfriend's jewellery. It's a good job you became aware of your dwindling finances before he got carried away. It would be best if you could get some concrete evidence of the unauthorised transactions before you get the police involved.'

Hannah stood up. 'So, my work here is done. I wish all my clients' needs were so simple.'

Toby rose from his chair. 'I'll need a lawyer now, won't I?'

Hannah looked at the floor, then the wall, anywhere without meeting his eyes. 'I would suggest so, once you've carried out the internal audit. I'm afraid I won't be available then,' Hannah crossed her fingers behind her back, 'I've got another client who's going to take up all of my time for the next few months.'

Toby watched as Hannah left his office, the vineyard and his life.

4

THE SNAGGING LIST

Hannah enlisted the help of her grandfather to produce a comprehensive snagging list concerning the building work undertaken on her house. So far, there were twenty-four issues.

'Am I being picky, Grandpa? Is the odd crack in a wall, or a wobbly floor tile just normal for a place as old as this? I do appreciate that I've not moved into a brand-new house and I've chosen to live on the side of a cliff, but I thought that I could make the interior look sleek and stylish without the plaster cracking within days of moving in.'

Arthur sighed. 'Well, Hannah, this building is very old. Just view the cracks as wrinkles. It'll be good for it to get its character back. It's a bit clinical at the moment. When AJ has kicked a few balls around and scuffed up the skirting boards, it'll feel more like home.'

Hannah was horrified, and Arthur's eyes twinkled. 'Your grandmother and I had a home full of fingerprints on the walls and dirty socks on the floor when you were all growing up, and that was just from the twins. A young boy will get into much more mess. I know I did.'

The doorbell rang, and Arthur made his escape. 'Perfect timing, I'm off to the pub to meet Clive. He hosted a posh do last night, and he's got some good ideas for our new school. Theo's joining us – let's hope he's got the pints in.'

Arthur opened the front door to let Rob Sharnbrook enter. He winked at the young man and whispered, 'Good luck, son, you could be here all week.'

Hannah called out, 'Come through to the kitchen, Rob, I've got the kettle on.' Hannah had placed the vase of wilting tulips on the kitchen table. As a lawyer, she didn't take any chances with conflicting information. She waited to see if there was a reaction from Rob.

'Nice flowers. Moving in gift from someone?'

Hannah crossed her fingers under the work surface. 'Yes. Although, I much prefer yellow roses.'

That was a blatant lie; yellow tulips were her favourites. Her mother had grown yellow tulips in the garden of the Solent Sea Guest House. There wasn't much Hannah remembered about her mother as she was only ten when she died. She did remember the tulips though.

Rob smiled brightly. 'What a coincidence so does my mother. I bought her yellow roses for her birthday last week.'

That wasn't a good start; lying to Rob. It would have mattered a couple of weeks ago, but now he seemed young and immature. He must be late twenties, and she was only thirty, but the glimmer of a spark that had developed over the winter had somehow extinguished.

The doorbell rang again, and Mrs Carruthers stood on the doorstep holding a large white box. 'Hannah, this has just arrived for you. I asked Tabitha to mind the shop for me while I popped up here so that you could open it. I wonder what it can be? I know for certain it's not that steam cleaner you've ordered. It's far too light.'

Mrs Carruthers caught sight of Rob. 'Oh, hello dear, did your wife like the flowers last week?'

Rob's ready smile lit up his face. 'I'm not married. The flowers were for my mother.'

Mrs Carruthers surveyed Rob in a different light. He was nice looking. His designer stubble was tidy enough, and his sandy hair and light blue eyes suited him. She didn't see him as a match for Hannah though. Hannah would eat him alive.

'Now, come along, Hannah. Open the box. We're waiting to see what's inside. Is there any chance of a cuppa? It's quite a climb up the High Street to get to you.'

Hannah made the teas and opened a packet of macaroons. It would be a long afternoon now that Mrs Carruthers had arrived. She'd already been on a tour of the house, with Rob in tow, and had now settled down in the living room on the sofa.

While her guests were in deep conversation, Hannah opened the box in the kitchen. Her hand flew to her mouth when she saw the ivory lace cocktail dress. There was a small box on top which, when opened, revealed an emerald bracelet. Hannah unfolded the note in the box.

Dear Hannah,

It will match your eyes, just make sure it doesn't snag on the dress. By the way, we have unfinished business.

Regards, Toby Finchinglake

Hannah felt excited, sick, guilty and mortified all rolled into one. She sealed the box up and handed it back to Mrs Carruthers. 'This box has been sent to the wrong address. I've put a new label on it. If you could forward it on that would be fantastic. Here's twenty pounds to cover the cost, if there's any change you can keep it for your trouble.'

Mrs Carruthers hadn't brought her glasses with her; Hannah's handwriting was quite small. She jumped up from the sofa and said her goodbyes. Back at the Post Office & General Store, she felt a sense of disappointment – the package was meant for Tobias Finchinglake at the vineyard. It would be nice if Hannah had a bit of romance in her life, and that wasn't going to happen with Rob, Mrs Carruthers was sure of it.

*

Two hours later Rob had inspected everything on the snagging list. 'These old buildings have a mind of their own. I'll do my best to make good for now. I'll need to come back with plaster and paint tomorrow . . .'

Hannah's head was thumping. How dare he send her that dress? How did he know her size? Shouldn't he know that an emerald bracelet was going too far? What would his wife say? What did he mean about "unfinished business"? She hadn't heard a word of what Rob was saying.

'. . . so it's a date then, I'll pick you up at seven, put your best dress on.'

Hannah was stunned back to reality. 'I can't go on a date, what about AJ?'

'Don't say you've forgotten already. You said your sister Matilda had taken him out for the day and he was staying at hers overnight to give you a break.'

Rob opened the front door. 'I'm not taking "no" for an answer. It's the least I can do to make up for all the snagging issues.'

5

A DEAL WITH THE FINCHINGLAKES

Rob held open the door to the King Arthur for Hannah to walk through. She couldn't believe she'd accepted to go on a date with him. It was the last thing she wanted. Why on earth hadn't she turned him down flat? The trouble was, her mind was elsewhere, and she couldn't think straight. She had to sort herself out, and quick.

Tabitha was behind the bar with Steve Copperfield. Hannah smiled and headed for a table as far away as possible while Rob went to order their drinks. Sitting next to the window overlooking the garden Hannah was surprised to see Fluffy outside. Rob sat down next to her. 'Tabitha says today's specials are seafood pie and chilli con carne. Are you OK eating here, or would you prefer to go to the bistro?'

'I just want something quick, so the chilli for me please.'

Rob stood up to place their order at the bar. 'Great choice, I'll go for the same. I'll be back in a minute.'

When Tabitha brought their meals over, Hannah enquired why Fluffy was in the garden.

'Oh, Grandpa asked if we'd keep an eye on him while he's at the vineyard with Clive and Theo.'

Hannah's heart raced. 'What are they doing at the vineyard?'

Tabitha shrugged her shoulders. 'No idea, you know what Grandpa's like, always in the thick of things. He's even worse when he gets involved with Clive. Can I get you anything to go with your chilli? Sour cream perhaps? Any parmesan?'

Hannah shook her head, and Rob jumped up. 'I'll pop up to the bar and order another pint. Hannah, are you OK with your wine? You've hardly touched it.' Hannah nodded, and Rob refused Tabitha's offer to bring his drink over.

Leaning on the bar, Rob watched Tabitha as she poured another pint. The overhead lights bounced off her long red curly hair and enhanced the sparkle in her emerald green eyes. Rob knew the Makepeace twins were attractive – he'd just not realised how much. Tabitha was full of life and worlds apart from Hannah who was lost in her thoughts. Rob doubted she'd even noticed he'd gone back up to the bar.

'Here's your pint. You'd better get back before your chilli goes cold.'

'Thanks, Tabitha, I wouldn't mind some parmesan if it's not too much trouble.'

'Of course, I'll bring some over.'

Hannah was pushing the food around on her plate when her sister arrived with the parmesan. 'Aren't you hungry, Hannah?'

Hannah put down her fork as the pub door opened and her grandfather, Clive and Theo walked in. 'I'm sorry, Rob, but this isn't working. I should never have said I'd go out with you. I have to go and catch up with the news on the vineyard. Make sure you're around in the morning to start clearing down that snagging list.'

Hannah pushed her chair back and went to join her grandfather's group. Tabitha was mortified, and Rob smiled. 'Well, you could say that I've been well and truly "dumped".' Tabitha sat down in Hannah's seat and drank her wine. How could her sister be so rude?

Lord Sonning-Smythe, Clive to his friends, was the principal investor in the village's renovations and the number one project currently on his list was to bring to life his best friend Arthur's dream of re-opening the village school.

Clive kissed Hannah on both cheeks, and she sat down at their table. 'What a coincidence seeing you, Hannah! You'll be the first to hear the exciting news about AJ's new school. I held an event last night at Sonning Hall for key business leaders in the south of England and, as luck would have it, Tobias Finchinglake turned up. He rarely attends such events. He's never been to one at the Hall before.'

Theo came back from the bar with a tray of drinks, he'd got a wine for Hannah, and she took a large gulp. Steve Copperfield was busy at the bar and glaring at Tabitha who was laughing at Rob's jokes.

Clive continued, 'It just so happens that Sophie Finchinglake is a qualified school teacher and she's been home-schooling the little Finchinglakes. When I mentioned our new school to Tobias, he said he was sure Sophie would be keen to teach at the school in Truelove Hills. She'd been concerned that Josie and Jules weren't interacting with other children and at six and seven that's not ideal – no fun in that. So that's where we've been this afternoon, getting Sophie Finchinglake to sign on the dotted line.'

Theo couldn't contain his news any longer. 'And that's not all, Hannah. Tobias Finchinglake has come up with a proposal for Truelove Hills to offer holiday packages with trips to his vineyard. It's a brilliant idea. We've signed up for that too!'

*

Hannah's bad mood continued for the next two days. She hardly said a word to Rob as he corrected all the issues on the snagging list, she just wanted him gone so that she could put that unfortunate "date" behind her. But that wasn't the main reason for the dark cloud that surrounded her; what terrible luck that Sophie Finchinglake was a school teacher. That meant Hannah would come across the Finchinglakes in some shape or form on a daily basis and the very thought made her heart sink.

There was only one way that Hannah could lift herself out of this hole, and that was to throw herself into work. Except there was no work. She'd advertised her services locally, but it was proving difficult to get her business off the ground.

The sound of the doorbell interrupted her thoughts. Mrs Carruthers was on the doorstep again – with another white box.

Rob laughed. 'What's inside that box? Is it a boomerang?'

Hannah took the box from Mrs Carruthers without inviting her in. She was in no mood for chatting to her, or to anyone.

*

That evening, when AJ was asleep, Hannah opened the box. This time it contained a different note.

Dear Hannah,

For a lawyer, your attention to detail is in question. Photographs in magazines mean nothing if you don't read the associated article. We had a deal, and you've broken it. Your punishment is to wear this dress on Saturday night and come to the vineyard for eight o'clock. If you wear the bracelet, that will show me you mean business, and I may forgive you for doing your best to bring your profession into disrepute.

Regards, Toby Finchinglake

Hannah's shaking hands dropped the note. Toby Finchinglake was both annoying and obnoxious. How did his wife tolerate him? Against her better judgement, she reached for her phone. 'Theo, it's me, I've got a business event on Saturday night, is there any chance that AJ can come and stay over at yours? That's great, Theo, thank Matilda for me. We'll see you soon.'

6

THE EMERALD BALL

Hannah decided to be late on Saturday night. There was no way she was going to take orders from that infuriating man. She wore the dress but not the bracelet and turned up at the vineyard for eight forty-five, to be met by the sight of a mass of people in black tie and evening dress, all seated and finishing the first course of their meal. A waiter showed her to a spare seat. Toby and Sophie were nowhere in sight.

The woman on her left flaunted her princess cut six-carat emerald ring. 'May I ask why you're so late for the Emerald Ball? You must know that tickets for this are scarce. Missing the start is simply taboo. Let's hope Tobias hasn't noticed. Why aren't you wearing emeralds?'

Hannah was speechless. She reached inside her clutch bag and clipped the bracelet around her wrist. The wine was flowing, and she numbed her embarrassment by drinking heartily. Many of the women were in ballgowns. So, from feeling very overdressed, Hannah now felt quite insignificant in a room full of taffeta, lace and emeralds.

Hannah nudged the man on her right. 'Have youuu, been to one of theeese before?'

The man smiled. 'We are fortunate enough to be invited every year. Donations to charity go a long way with getting tickets. The only condition is that all the ladies wear emeralds – they're Mr Finchinglake's favourite stone.'

Hannah stared at her bracelet. 'Why's that?'

'Emeralds are stones of great vision and intuition, long believed to foretell future events and reveal one's truths.'

Hannah giggled, surely Toby didn't believe all that nonsense. 'Soooo, where is Mr Finchinglake now?'

The man nodded towards a balcony in the barn just as everyone stood up and clinked their glasses before chanting Toby's name.

Toby smiled and gestured for everyone to sit down. 'Once again, I would like to thank you all for participating in our annual Emerald Ball. This year, all proceeds will be going to nursing homes within a thirty-mile radius of the vineyard, in honour of Billy Tomlin, a former much-loved resident of the Truelove Hills community. I will now hand you over to Billy's grandson, Will Tomlin, who will conduct tonight's auction.'

Hannah signalled for another wine to be poured. The auction was at Lot 36 before it caught her attention. 'And now we have a 1920s aerial shot of the cliff on the west coast of Truelove Hills. Who will give me £100?'

Several hands shot up. The bidding was coming to a close at £5,000 when Hannah decided to take part. She waved her hand furiously.

'That's £6,000 from the lady at the far end of the room.'

Toby noticed Hannah swaying in the distance, and he bid against her to save her embarrassment.

'Now we have a bid of £7,000.'

Hannah waved her arm again.

'£8,000 to the lady.'

Toby tried to diffuse the situation. '£10,000 to the man.'

Hannah signalled to Will Tomlin by holding up her handful of fingers five times.

'The lady wants to pay £15,000 for the photograph. Are there any further bidders? Going once, going twice . . . gone!'

*

Hannah stretched out her legs; the sheets felt cool and smooth. She stretched her arms and felt the sun on her face. She daren't open her eyes. She didn't know where she was – or who she was with. She was a mess. A total and utter mess. She opened an eyelid. There was no-one around, so she opened the other and sat up in the bed. There was a black and white photograph propped up on the dressing table and a note that read: *"You owe me £15,000."*

Hannah squirmed and downed the glass of water on the bedside table. A knock came on the door, and Toby enquired, 'May I come in?'

Hannah pulled a sheet around her and whimpered, 'Yes'.

Toby was carrying a breakfast tray full of food. 'I thought we could have breakfast together while we talked business. You wore the bracelet last night to signify that you mean business, am I correct?' Hannah nodded.

'Well, I now know why you bid so fiercely for that photograph. It's incriminating evidence against my family. I admire you for that. I hadn't spotted the significance before.'

Toby poured the orange juice. 'I suggest that after breakfast I drive you home. Who looked after AJ last night?'

'My sister and brother-in-law. I'm so fortunate to have my family all around me.'

Toby touched Hannah's hand. 'You were wrong about Will using my money to buy presents for his girlfriend. He confessed to me that he needed the money to pay for his grandfather's funeral. He's paid the money back now. It was just a loan.'

Hannah felt a lump in her throat. 'It was very kind of you to give the proceeds of last night's charity event to local nursing homes in memory of Billy Tomlin.'

'It was the least I could do. Will's a good employee. I like to help out if I can. He only needed to ask for a loan in the first place. Still, if he hadn't chosen to be devious, I wouldn't have needed your services.'

Hannah's face dropped. 'I suppose that means my work at the vineyard really is done. You won't need a private investigator now that you can trust your accountant again.'

Toby smiled. 'I'll always need a lawyer though, and you're my Lawyer of Choice.'

*

The pedestrianised High Street in Truelove Hills only granted access to VIP's, emergency vehicles and residents. The wheels of Toby's Range Rover crunched up the drive to Hannah's house and stopped by the front door.

Hannah clutched the photograph and was keen to get inside to scrutinise it to establish what Toby had discovered. She'd only started bidding for it because her house was in it. Unfortunately, due to the delicious Finchinglake wine, and the desire not to lose to Toby, she'd got carried away.

The emerald bracelet on Hannah's arm glistened in the sunlight. Toby looked her in the eyes. 'Are you planning on keeping the bracelet?'

Hannah held her arm up in the air. 'Too right I am! I'll view it as a bonus for establishing that photograph is gold dust. See you soon, Tobias Finchinglake. I'll be in touch!'

7

AN INCRIMINATING PHOTOGRAPH

The aerial shot gave a sweeping view of Pebble Cove, the cliffs and Hannah's house. Until Hannah had undertaken the renovation work over the winter, there wasn't much change in the black and white photograph to the present day – one hundred years on.

There was a boat moored against the shoreline at Pebble Cove, and Hannah squinted to make out the writing on the side, it read: "FINCHY". There was another boat heading south along the coastline with the name: "MARY MOON". There were two people in the second boat; one was lying down, and the other's long hair was flying behind her as she held onto the oars. Why was the photograph incriminating evidence against the Finchinglakes?

Hannah popped in to see her grandfather on her way down the High Street to collect AJ. She was intrigued about the history of her new home.

'Grandpa, did Billy Tomlin ever mention his ancestors to you?'

Arthur signalled for Hannah to take a seat while he collected his thoughts. 'Well now, it's a sure fact that his family were staff at the castle for many a generation and lived in your house. There's a bit of mystery as well – there used to be smugglers coming into Pebble Cove with precious goods.'

Hannah wasn't shocked in the slightest. 'Well, Pebble Cove many years back would have been a hive of activity with smugglers bringing illegal alcohol and tobacco up those ninety-nine steps into my kitchen. That's what happened in those days. Thank goodness there's no risk of that now I've had the walkway built down the side of the cliff.' Hannah winked at her grandfather.

Arthur sighed and considered his words carefully. 'There were all sorts of dodgy dealings going on in the olden days. It was a way of life around these parts. There was even a rumour, when I was a boy, that the Finchinglakes had contraband and guns if anyone stood in their way. That's our secret though, Hannah, we don't want anything harming the good relationship we have now between the Finchinglakes and Truelove Hills.'

Hannah was used to her grandfather's colourful stories. 'So, what type of illegal goods were the Finchinglakes dealing in?'

Arthur looked Hannah straight in the eyes. 'Emeralds.'

*

Hannah was keen to hear Toby's side of the story, so she took the photograph to the vineyard. 'Why is this photograph incriminating evidence against your family?'

'Did you notice the names on the boats?'

Hannah lowered her eyes. 'I presume that "FINCHY" is short for "Finchinglake".'

Toby paced around his office. 'That boat was stolen from my great-grandfather. Our family name was nearly destroyed by the rumours that went around at that time. My great-grandfather was hanged for the murder of Josiah Tomlin at Pebble Cove even though a body was never found. Did you see the name on the other boat, the one being rowed by a woman with a corpse in it?'

Hannah's eyes widened – the person lying down

was dead? 'The boat's name was "MARY MOON".'

'That was my great-grandmother's maiden name. Did she murder Josiah Tomlin and let my great-grandfather take the blame? Or was she his accomplice and disposed of the body?'

Hannah wrung her hands together before pushing the photograph across Toby's desk. 'You should keep this. My first thought was that the person was lying down, not that it was a dead body.'

Toby opened a drawer in his desk and pulled out a magnifying glass. He scrutinised the photograph. 'You're right, Hannah, the man's staring at my great-grandmother and he's clutching onto bags. He's not dead. I always knew my great-grandfather was innocent.'

Hannah stood up. 'Innocent of murder, maybe, but what about smuggling?'

Toby hesitated and stared out of his office window for several seconds before turning to face Hannah. 'This is between you and me, not even Sophie knows, there's a chest of emeralds in a vault under this building. My father and grandfather never mentioned them, and I don't know what to do with them.'

Hannah was humbled that Toby would trust her with such a secret. 'Is the emerald connection why you hold an annual Emerald Ball? Is it your way of putting right your ancestor's wrongs in the best and only way you can?'

Toby lowered his eyes. 'Yes.'

*

Toby chose to meet Theo and Hannah at Chateau Amore de Pebblio to discuss the legalities of the joint venture between Finchinglake Vineyard and Truelove Hills. Hannah was curious why the meeting wasn't held at the vineyard and why Toby's behaviour towards her was professional and remote.

'So, Hannah, if you could get the contracts drawn up, I'd be grateful if you would email them to me for approval and I'll post the signed copies back to you so that Theo can sign on behalf of Truelove Hills.'

Toby strode across the car park, and Hannah made an excuse to Theo about having to rush after him.

'Toby, what's wrong? If it's to do with your family's history, then you can trust me not to mention it to anyone. I'm your lawyer and . . . and a friend.'

'That's just the point, Hannah, the burden of my family's past is for me to suffer alone. I should never have confided in you, and I certainly don't want Sophie finding out. It's best we keep things on a professional basis in future. I apologise for concerning you with my problems. I'll keep the photograph locked away and pay the £15,000 to the Emerald Ball fund. That's the best solution.'

'But, Toby . . . '

Toby stared into Hannah's glistening emerald eyes before bending down to kiss her on the cheek. 'Another time, another place, Hannah, and things would have been different between us. With the black cloud that surrounds me, there's no room for a relationship. It's something I will live with for the rest of my life.'

'But, you're married, Toby. You should be able to confide in Sophie.'

Toby wound down his car window. 'I never said I was married. Sophie is my sister.'

Hannah stood holding her cheek as she watched Toby's car drive slowly away from the chateau.

8

HOUSING FOR EVERYONE

With the school renovation well underway, Clive had already identified future investment opportunities and sat in the pub divulging his ideas to Arthur.

'Hannah's been very kind to show me the tremendous work the builders have undertaken on her property. I believe we should make more use of the coastline adjacent to Truelove Hills. I've got contacts who will get the planning permission through. It won't be cheap, but I can visualise renovating the properties on the cliff to the south of Hannah's house. Once we've got an access road down there, we could either sell them or rent them out as holiday lets. With those properties and the ones in the hills that are undergoing renovation, there will be quite a selection of available housing soon.'

Arthur nodded his approval while he gathered his thoughts. 'What's going to happen when Cindy has your grandchild? She's due next month. Cindy needs a nice house if she's going to be bringing up a little one. That apartment above her businesses won't be any good. It's large enough, but it hasn't got a garden. Is your son going to be spending more time on this side of the world once he's a father? Cindy will need him around.'

Clive smiled. 'There's no need to worry, Arthur, Jamie's every bit as keen to play a part in the baby's life, as am I. He's taking on a lesser role in his company which will free him up to spend more time at home.'

Arthur asked the dreaded question that had been bothering him for months. 'They're not going to live with you at Sonning Hall, are they? Cindy belongs to Truelove Hills.'

Clive's eyes twinkled; he'd been waiting for his friend's reproach. 'Cindy's made it very clear to Jamie that she won't be leaving Truelove Hills for the long term and I quite agree with her. Why would she want to live in a big empty house when all her friends are here? We have agreed that, when the baby is born, Cindy and Jamie will stay at the Hall until a property is available for them in Truelove Hills.'

Arthur signalled to Bruce Copperfield to bring over two more pints before expressing his relief. 'That's good news, Clive. We'd best crack on with the building work then, Matilda and Theo will need a house soon. They can't bring up a family living above her shop.'

*

The sign on the door of Matilda's Memorabilia had been turned from "OPEN" to "CLOSED" for three days in a row. Not for the whole of the day – just until eleven o'clock in the mornings. Arthur was surprised that his son hadn't mentioned it. The shop was opposite the Solent Sea Guest House. Still, David Makepeace had never been one for gossip. He kept himself to himself.

Mrs Carruthers was another matter. She'd mentioned it to Arthur on Tuesday, Wednesday and Thursday. Arthur wasn't one to delve into people's private lives, but Matilda was his granddaughter, and he'd made a point of popping into her shop every afternoon this week to enquire how the pebblestone artefacts he'd made were selling. The heart-shaped pebbles were always popular, but only three fruit bowls had been sold in the last month.

Matilda looked up from her seat behind the counter. 'Not *you*, again, Grandpa. What have I done to deserve all this attention? You normally only pop into the shop when you're bringing something new for me to sell, not for daily updates.'

'Well, I have a bit of news you might be interested in, Tilly. Clive's going to renovate some seafront properties on the cliff south of Hannah's. I wanted you and Theo to know first, as Cindy and Jamie are looking for a house too. I don't know if they'll go for the hills or the cliff. As you're all best friends, it's good timing that you can bring your families up together right here in the village.'

Arthur winked and headed for the door. Matilda glared at him as he crossed the road. Her grandfather was looking more energetic than usual. He'd guessed that she was pregnant and she hadn't even told Theo yet.

*

Two weeks later, Rob Sharnbrook decided to celebrate the news of more building work by inviting Tabitha for dinner at Cindy's Bistro. Tabitha didn't hesitate in accepting his offer. It was slightly awkward since Cindy had hoped her brother, Steve, and Tabitha would become an item, but the connection just wasn't there like it was with Rob.

With both Steve and Bruce Copperfield working in the pub and Tallulah happy to cover Tabitha's shift, a date at the bistro would be uninterrupted. Heavily pregnant Cindy had already given up the evening shifts with just ten days to go.

Tabitha wore her best cream dress and clipped her long red curls up on one side. She'd pleaded with her sister, Hannah, to borrow the emerald bracelet she always wore these days but to no avail, so she cut a length of emerald ribbon and tied it in her hair to bring out the colour of her eyes.

By the end of the first course, Rob reached across the table to hold her hand. Tabitha jumped slightly. Her gaze hadn't left Rob's since they'd chosen from the menu. There was a magnetism she hadn't experienced before, and she was oblivious that Matilda and Theo had entered the room and were now sitting at a table by the window.

Theo held onto Tilly's hand. 'How are you feeling, has the sickness subsided? I can't wait until we tell everyone our news.'

The bistro door opened to the sight of Tallulah. She walked up to the bar area and asked if she could borrow a jar of olives as the pub had run out. She ordered a cider while she was there and climbed up onto a bar stool. The next person to enter the bistro was Steve Copperfield. He skulked in staring at Tabitha out of the corner of his eye. Steve sat at the bar next to Tallulah and ordered a whisky.

Matilda didn't know whether to laugh or cry. 'Oh, poor Steve, he's well and truly lost his chance with Tabitha. She's not even noticed he's here – she's not noticed any of us are here. Trust Tallulah to come over to spy on her sister. Poor Bruce is left running the pub on his own.'

Mrs Carruthers was next to enter the bistro. She peered around the door, waved to Matilda and Theo, then pulled out a chair and sat down at their table. 'What's going on? There's a queue in the pub, so I thought I'd pop in here for a drink.' She signalled to a waiter. 'Double brandy for me please.'

Theo's phone flashed. 'Please excuse me. I need to pop outside and take this call.' Matilda checked to see that her phone was off. Theo usually did the same. She glanced at Tabitha and Rob at the table in the middle of the room. She guessed their phones were turned off if they'd even remembered bringing them.

A piercing scream shattered the ambience in the bistro just as Bruce Copperfield charged through the door. 'Am I the only person with a phone switched on? Cindy's gone into labour!'

Cindy staggered into the room, and Steve and Bruce ran over to help their sister onto a chair. Theo rushed into the bistro behind Bruce. He phoned Jamie back. 'I must say, your timing's perfect. How far away are you now? Ten minutes? Cindy's gone into labour.'

9

A PRESENT FOR MUMMY

Clive ensured the nursery at Sonning Hall was decorated to the standard befitting of his first grandchild. He'd sent the Bentley to the hospital to collect Cindy, Jamie and baby Sebastian Sonning-Smythe and waited at the doorway of the Hall to welcome them. The trees that lined the drive were tied with blue ribbons, and balloons decorated the hallway and sweeping staircase.

'Welcome! Welcome!'

Cindy handed Sebastian to his grandfather, and Jamie ushered her into the drawing room to be met by the sight of flowers, cuddly toys and her best friend, Matilda, who was joined by Hannah, AJ, Mrs Carruthers and Arthur.

Clive beamed at Cindy's delight. 'I couldn't get the

whole of Truelove Hills here to meet little Sebastian today. It's such a busy village now that there's work to attend to at all times. Your brothers are both coming to the Hall tomorrow for when your parents arrive.' Mr & Mrs Copperfield had retired to Spain and were most appreciative of Clive's offer to spend as long as they wanted at Sonning Hall to meet little Sebastian.

Jamie's excitement was infectious. AJ stood in the hallway and watched as the new father ran up the stairs two at a time and returned within minutes holding a small blue box tied with white ribbon. Jamie held a finger to his lips and patted AJ's head. 'It's a present for Sebastian's Mummy.'

Jamie handed his wife the gift. 'I meant to bring this to the hospital, Cindy, but with all the excitement over the last couple of days, I forgot. Here's a little present for Mummy from Sebastian.'

Cindy opened the box to reveal a blue topaz and diamond necklace. 'It's beautiful, Jamie.'

Jamie grinned. 'Don't thank me, thank Sebastian. I'm sure it will be the first of many gifts from your son.'

Clive's staff served afternoon tea with champagne for any partakers. Mrs Carruthers was on her third glass when she noticed AJ climbing up the stairs. Was no-one keeping an eye on that boy? Glass in hand she followed him. She whispered, 'AJ, wait for me, you shouldn't be going up the stairs on your own.' Mrs Carruthers looked over her shoulder; no-one was paying any attention – they were all cooing over the baby. She wouldn't mind seeing what Sonning Hall was like upstairs, so she let AJ lead the way.

There were several floors, and AJ was determined to climb until he reached the top of the building. Mrs Carruthers was out of breath. She'd put her glass down on an occasional table on the third-floor landing, if the boy didn't stop soon, she'd have to call for help to catch him. At the top of the stairs, Mrs Carruthers sat down on the nearest chair. It wouldn't hurt for AJ to have a run around up here, as long as she made sure he didn't try to get down the stairs on his own.

AJ ran down the corridors pushing all the doors on his way, but they were either locked or just too heavy for him to open. The sun was shining through a window at the end of one of the corridors, and a shard of green sparkle attracted AJ's attention. It was the same sparkle that his Mummy's bracelet made. AJ climbed on a chair and lifted the small green box from a windowsill.

Mrs Carruthers stopped AJ in his tracks. 'Now give that to me, we need to put the box back where you got it from.'

AJ clutched the box with all his might and rolled around on the floor crying, 'Present for Mummy!'

There was no other way to get the boy downstairs but to let him hold onto the box. Hannah could prise it off him when they got back to the drawing room.

Hannah was horrified. 'AJ! Let go of the box. It doesn't belong to us; it belongs to Clive. I'm so sorry, Clive.'

Clive held out his hands, and AJ reluctantly gave him the box. 'That's a good boy. I can quite see why you like the box it matches your mother's bracelet. They're both rather pretty aren't they?'

AJ wiped his eyes on his sleeve. 'Present for Mummy.'

Clive handed the box back to AJ. 'You have excellent taste, AJ. I haven't seen this box for years. The staff move things around quite a lot. I have no need for it, and as you have shown a fondness for it, then it would give me no greater pleasure than for you to keep it.'

AJ hugged Clive and Hannah's protests were ignored.

*

Hannah didn't know whether to be annoyed with AJ or heartened that he wanted to give her a present. She just knew she was embarrassed to now have an emerald box from Sonning Hall sitting on her kitchen windowsill. She'd put it up there so that AJ couldn't reach it. When the sun caught it, shards of green sparkle bounced off the white worktops and units. It had been dark when they got home yesterday and a very late night for AJ. Hannah wasn't surprised he was having a lie in this morning.

Hannah was sitting at the kitchen table, drinking her coffee in uninterrupted silence when curiosity got the better of her. AJ had said the box didn't open in the car on the way home, but what was the point of a box that didn't open? Hannah lifted the box off the windowsill and retrieved a steak knife from the cutlery drawer to prise the lid open, to her surprise it opened straight away. There was a gold key inside and gold initials painted on the cream satin lining of the lid: "MM".

AJ was awake. Hannah placed the key back in the box and returned it to the windowsill.

'Mummy, I want juice and toast.'

'What's the magic word, AJ?'

'Pleeeeease, Mummy!'

10

NAMING OF THE SCHOOL

Mrs Carruthers was beside herself. Clive had given her one job to do, and it was turning into a disaster. She was responsible for gaining public support in the naming of the school. As a pillar of the community, Mrs Carruthers was best placed to do this, but she'd put a simple procedure in place that had spectacularly backfired.

The deadline for the shortlist of names was tonight. Mrs Carruthers had been invited to dinner at the pub with Clive and Arthur before the official announcement.

Mrs Carruthers twisted her serviette on her lap. It was disintegrating fast. Tallulah noticed and brought her another one, along with a double brandy. 'What's up, Mrs Carruthers? You look flustered. I bet you've got lots of good names for the school tucked up your sleeve. It's only Grandpa and Clive you've got to give the shortlist of names to. Has anyone come up with any good ones? Go on, you can tell me.'

Mrs Carruthers shook her head and waved Tallulah away before sipping her brandy, she had to be able to articulate the procedure she'd followed after being given such an important task. Arthur opened the door to the pub and Mrs Carruthers saw Clive's gleaming black Bentley outside. She downed her brandy. Tallulah laughed. 'Let me take that empty glass for you. I'll get you another drink.'

Tallulah was keen to stay within earshot. Something was bothering Mrs Carruthers. What was so difficult about naming a school?

Clive kissed Mrs Carruthers on both cheeks. 'I must say I am keen to know the suggested names the residents have come up with for the school. How did you gain their support in proposing ideas?'

Mrs Carruthers wiped her brow with her serviette. 'Well, it wasn't easy. I had an anonymous suggestion box on the Post Office counter.'

Clive rubbed his hands together. 'I'm very interested to know what the anonymous suggestions are.'

Mrs Carruthers bent down and pulled out a sheet

of paper from her bag. 'We had five suggestions. I've written them down on here.'

Clive read the names then passed the sheet of paper to Arthur who ripped it up before glaring at Mrs Carruthers. 'We've given you one job to do, and all you've come up with is a list of obscenities.'

Mrs Carruthers held her shoulders back. 'It's nothing to do with me. There were some young boys in the shop last week. My guess is the suggestions came from them.'

Tallulah sniggered as she cleared a nearby table and Clive looked at his watch. 'I suggest we order our meals. We have less than an hour until the residents arrive to hear the chosen name of the school.'

Mrs Carruthers tucked into her burger and chips, and Clive was thoughtful. Arthur nudged him. 'What are we going to do? There'll be a fair few people here tonight, all of my family are coming.'

Clive sliced through his steak with peppercorn sauce before wiping his mouth on a serviette. 'Don't worry, Arthur. I have the perfect solution. Things could not have turned out better.'

Clive summoned Tallulah over and whispered in her ear. Tallulah rushed over to the bar to speak to her father. 'Clive's said to give everyone champagne so that they can toast the name of the school.'

David Makepeace raised his bushy black eyebrows. 'Any idea what they're calling it?'

Tallulah shook her head. 'I don't think they have either.'

The pub was full by the time Matilda and Theo arrived. The smiles on their faces spoke volumes. Arthur called them over. 'Have you got some news for us?'

Theo clasped his wife's hand. 'Tilly and I are expecting. Baby Tressler is due in December.'

Arthur winked at his granddaughter. 'I'd already worked that one out.'

Matilda laughed. 'There's nothing that gets past you, Grandpa. We need to tell the others.' Soon the whole Makepeace family were chatting excitedly at the bar.

Clive stood up and clapped his hands. 'We have just received some splendid news. Another Truelove Hills baby is on the way.' There were raised eyebrows in the crowd and Theo waved his hand high in the air to the sound of cheers and whistles around the room. Clive continued, 'Another little one to go to our new school: the Alice Makepeace Academy.'

There was a stunned silence before the room erupted with wholehearted approval. The Makepeace family smiled through their tears. Clive grinned at Arthur, and Mrs Carruthers was aghast. 'Who came up with that name? It wasn't in the suggestion box.'

Clive's eyes twinkled. 'It was a last-minute entrant. A perfect one I might add. It's important that the key buildings in the village that give it its heart are named after eminent local individuals. The pub's named after Arthur and now the school's named after his beloved wife, Alice.'

Mrs Carruthers was annoyed with herself for missing an opportunity. The "Mrs Carruthers Community College" was an idea that suddenly sprang to mind. Too late now, though.

On his way home, Arthur looked to the sky. 'Well now, Alice, another great-grandchild on the way and the new school being named after you all in one day. I know you'll be thrilled to bits! I've got a bit of bother going on in my mind at the moment. There's something funny about all these emeralds turning up. Hannah's only been wearing that bracelet since we started dealing with the Finchinglakes, and now AJ's found that box. Don't worry; I'll get to the bottom of it.'

11

BARBECUE AT PEBBLE COVE

Tallulah moaned as she helped carry the provisions down the side of the cliff. She sat down on one of the benches and took in the sea view. Theo sat down next to her. 'I've got an idea, Theo, next time Hannah decides to have a party on the beach we can hire a boat, drive down to where it's moored, hop on with all the food and sail over to Pebble Cove.'

Theo laughed. 'That's a great idea, Tallulah, but I've got a better one.'

'Go on then, Theo, tell me *your* grand plan.'

'You can drive down to Matilda's house with everything you need in the boot of your car. When we've loaded it onto my boat, we can all sail north up the coast to Pebble Cove.'

Tallulah snorted. 'You're so funny, Theo. Full marks for your imagination though.'

Theo turned to face his sister-in-law. 'I'm serious, Tallulah. I'm hoping to buy Matilda one of the houses by the sea that Clive's investing in. They're not as high up the cliff as Hannah's, and there will be a road direct to the beach. That's our secret though – I haven't told Tilly yet in case it all falls through. Do you think I'm doing the right thing?'

Tallulah shielded her eyes from the sun. 'Definitely! I want a "Theo". How lucky is my sister?'

Arthur was fishing in the rockpools with AJ. 'I used to do this with my friend, Billy Tomlin. When you start school in September, you'll have some little friends. That'll be good AJ, won't it?'

'Yes, Grandpa. Mummy says I can bring friends home for tea.'

'That's my boy, exciting times ahead for you.'

'I found a key, Grandpa.'

'Where, AJ? I can't see a key.'

'In the sparkly box. Mummy doesn't know. Look, Grandpa, a crab!'

Tabitha had invited Rob Sharnbrook to the barbecue, and he was turning out to be a most helpful guest. He'd run up and down the steps to the beach several times carrying planks of wood from one of the building sites to provide a makeshift decking area for Hannah's foldaway table and chairs. 'These are off-cuts of wood, Hannah, they'd only be scrapped, but at least the table and chairs will be on solid ground.'

'That's great, Rob. I'm going to store everything under the house so that we don't need to carry it all down next time. Having a door that leads straight from the beach to the basement of my property will be quite handy. Living in a smuggler's hideaway has some advantages!'

Matilda opened the door in the cliff face and wandered inside. She loved this house. How wonderful would it be to live next to the sea? This basement room could be used for all sorts of things; shelter when it rained; a changing area before swimming; a romantic candlelit dining room with sea view. Matilda sat on the steps that led down from the house and closed her eyes to imagine what life would have been like living here hundreds of years ago.

'Food's ready!'

Matilda was jolted from her thoughts. She opened her eyes and caught a glimpse of something tangled up in a small pile of seaweed and driftwood at the bottom of the steps. She pulled it free – it was a rusty old brooch with some murky green stones.

'Hannah! Look what I've found, do you think it's smugglers' treasure?'

Hannah strode into the basement and took the brooch from her sister. She made out the shape of the rusty initials, and her heart flipped. She crossed her fingers behind her back. 'Oh, thanks for finding this, Matilda. Lady Leticia asked me to look out for it. She dropped it down here one day. She'll be delighted to have it back. Come along now. Let's eat before the food goes cold. I've heard a rumour that Theo may be buying you your very own seaside retreat for when baby Tressler comes along.'

Theo's plan was a secret no longer. Tallulah was the worst person to confide in. Still, the news that one of Clive's new cliffside properties was going to Matilda and Theo turned the barbecue into a celebration. Tabitha turned up the music, and Rob was the centre of attention being bombarded with questions from all directions: 'How long will the building work take?'; 'Will the house be ready for when the baby arrives?'; 'Are there any other buyers for the seaside homes?'

Three others joined the group. Cindy, Jamie and Sebastian had arrived later than planned. Cindy gave their apologies. 'Sorry, everyone, getting out on time with a baby is impossible.' Jamie carried Sebastian in a sling, and he held up a bottle of champagne before pulling his smiling wife towards him. 'Cindy and I have been looking at the plans for the homes by the sea, and now that we know our best friends are buying one, we'll definitely sign up! Champagne everyone?'

The mould and rust on the brooch seeped through the material of Hannah's white linen shorts, she discretely removed it and wrapped it in a paper serviette before replacing it in her pocket. She'd need to return the brooch to its rightful owners, and that meant a trip to the vineyard in the morning.

*

The sun was setting by the time the party drew to a close, and Arthur offered to take AJ back to the house via the illuminated staggered walkway up the side of the cliff. AJ held his great-grandfather's hand all the way up and pulled him into the house as soon as Arthur unlocked the door.

'AJ's time for bed. Grandpa read story.'

Arthur patted AJ on the head. 'Mummy's on her way up to give you a quick bath first, but before she gets here, do you know where that sparkly box is, the one with the key?'

AJ rubbed his eyes and pointed to the kitchen. Arthur could see the box sitting on the kitchen windowsill. The sound of voices and "goodbyes" could be heard outside the front door and, when AJ wasn't looking, Arthur walked into the kitchen, reached into the box and removed the key.

Tabitha and Tallulah came looking for their grandfather and linked arms with him. 'Come on Grandpa. We'll see you get home safely.'

The weight of the key in Arthur's trouser pocket was minimal, but the weight on his mind was immense.

12

VISIT TO THE VINEYARD

It was ten o'clock the following morning when Hannah climbed out of her car and rang Toby's doorbell. There was no response. She'd left her car door open as AJ was in the back and she wasn't planning on stopping long. Hannah looked through the windows and around the sides of the property before returning to her car and unfastening AJ's car seat.

The vineyard workers were unable to shed light on Toby's whereabouts. 'We haven't seen Mr Toby today. You could check if Miss Sophie's home. That's her house over there.'

Hannah knew there were two houses on the site; she just hadn't put two and two together before to realise that Toby lived separately from his sister. Hannah strode down the driveway, pulling AJ behind. The house was newly-built, and Hannah glanced around it before ringing the doorbell. Sophie answered straight away.

'Hannah! How lovely to see you both. Please come in. AJ can meet Josie and Jules.'

Sophie's light brown hair was piled on top of her head with a paintbrush holding it in place. She noticed Hannah's wide-eyed amazement.

'I'm a teacher. We use pencils and paintbrushes all the time for everything. I believe in making imaginations run riot! I'm so excited about the school opening in September. I've got lots of ideas to bring the best out of the pupils and set them on their paths of fulfilment.'

The thud of feet on the stairs soon revealed two little Finchinglakes. A little girl, slightly taller than a little boy, both with light brown hair now stood in the hallway. Sophie sat on the floor and encouraged the children to join her. 'Who can see a paintbrush anywhere? The first to find it gets to choose if I should wear bright green wellie boots or flip flops when I go for a walk by the river in the mud.'

AJ's hearty chuckles were infectious, and he pointed to Sophie's hair. 'Well done, AJ, you found the paintbrush. Now, should I wear my wellies or flip flops if I'm going for a muddy walk?'

AJ laughed. 'Wellieeees!!!'

Sophie removed the paintbrush to let her long hair fall around her shoulders. 'Here you go, AJ, the paintbrush is your prize, you've saved me from getting dirty feet next time I go for a muddy walk. Thank you so much!'

AJ giggled, and Josie grabbed his hand. 'Come upstairs with us. You can see our bedrooms. We've got goldfish and wigwams and lots of pretty lights that come out at night. Mummy! Can AJ stay for a sleepover?'

Sophie laughed, and Hannah kept an eye on the stairs, to witness a uniformed nanny walking down them. 'If AJ's Mummy doesn't mind, maybe you can all become friends this morning, and then, at a later stage, AJ can come to stay with us for a sleepover.'

There were three cheers of 'Yessss!!!' as the children bounded past the nanny, and off up the stairs.

Hannah felt at ease with Sophie and her undoubted control of their children. 'Well, if I ever need a childminder then I know where to come, although I'm very fortunate having all of my family around me, there's always someone wanting to look after AJ. Anyway, the reason I came to the vineyard this morning was to speak to your brother. Do you know where he is?'

Sophie shook her head. 'I'm sorry you've had a wasted journey, come with me into the kitchen, and we can at least have a tea or coffee while the children are playing upstairs.'

The lounge was opposite the kitchen, and Hannah's eyes were drawn to the painting above the fireplace. She stood in the doorway taking in every detail.

Sophie called from the kitchen. 'Tea or coffee, Hannah? I know that painting doesn't look right in such a new house, but Toby was going to throw it out last week. Somehow my brother's taken a sudden dislike to our great-grandmother. I'm amazed at how his mind works. It's beyond me to question why.'

Hannah finished her coffee before calling for AJ. He descended the stairs hand-in-hand with the Finchinglake's nanny, counting every step he touched. 'We'll be off now, Sophie. Thank you for your hospitality this morning. I'll catch up with your brother some other time.'

*

Will Tomlin climbed out of his car as Hannah and AJ reached the car park. 'Hannah! It's great to see you. I was just asking Toby if you're going to be doing any more work for us. We haven't seen you for a while.'

'What did he say?'

'He said there was nothing planned.'

A white transit van skidded to a halt next to Will, and the bearded driver leant out of the window. 'Is Finchinglake around? I've been trying to track him down for days. If he keeps avoiding me, I'll take him to court!'

Hannah stepped forward. 'My name's Hannah Makepeace. I'm Mr Finchinglake's lawyer. If you have any legal issues concerning Mr Finchinglake, then you need to speak to me.'

'Do I need to book an appointment?'

'I'll see you at two o'clock the day after tomorrow in my office at Chateau Amore de Pebblio. Are you aware of the location?'

'Oh, yes. I'm well aware of it.'

The van sped off down the drive, and Will stared at Hannah. 'Don't worry, Will, I've got this. Toby doesn't need to be bogged down with trivia. I'll get to the bottom of Mr … er … the man's issues.'

Hannah strapped AJ into her car and jumped in – what was she doing? She hadn't even asked the van driver's name.

*

Toby was enjoying his latest venture. The club was due to open in two days' time. The staff were first rate, the kitchen was fully equipped, and the supply of fresh produce was arriving tomorrow. The bar had an extensive stock of beverages, and most importantly all the games were in place and had been tried and tested.

'I'd like to thank you all for coming in today for a final run through before we open. Please help yourselves to a bottle of wine on the way out. There's a choice of sparkling, red or white. Enjoy a glass with your families! I'll see you again at our official opening.'

*

The weight on Hannah's shoulders was immense – she wished she'd never set eyes on Toby Finchinglake. First, there was the photograph, then the brooch and now a painting that she couldn't get out of her mind. On top of all of that, she wanted to protect him, even by stupidly arranging an appointment with an anonymous man. She had become embroiled in the Finchinglake's dark past, and she was now trapped beyond all measure.

13

HELP FROM GRANDPA

Hannah was disturbed, and the only person she could turn to was her grandfather. She knocked on the door of his pebblestone cottage and waited on the pavement conscious of Mrs Carruthers' eyes burning into her back from the Post Office & General Store opposite.

Arthur was surprised to find his eldest granddaughter in such a state. 'What's happened, Hannah? There's nothing that's upset you for as long as I can remember, you've always been so strong.'

Arthur handed Hannah his handkerchief, and she blew her nose. Fluffy jumped up at her legs, and she sat down in the window seat of her grandfather's cottage to cradle his little white dog. 'I always thought I knew what was going on, Grandpa. You know, some sort of instinct. It's got me to where I am today, and I've always trusted it.'

Arthur nodded. 'Go on, Hannah, let it all out.'

'Well, since I've been back in Truelove Hills, events have overtaken me. I feel out of control, and I've been telling less than the truth just to get by.'

Arthur put a coaster on his windowsill and placed a cup of hot chocolate on top of it. Hannah wailed, and Arthur put his arm around her. 'You're never too old to tell your grandfather a secret or two. How many secrets have I kept over the years? If you need anyone to trust, it's me. I'll keep your secrets to the grave.'

Hannah spilt all. 'I'm in love with Toby Finchinglake.'

The news wasn't a surprise to Arthur. 'I see. You do remember what I told you about the Finchinglakes being involved with smuggling emeralds and using guns? They murdered Josiah Tomlin at Pebble Cove.'

Hannah held her head in her hands. 'Grandpa, Josiah Tomlin escaped. His body was never found. He wasn't murdered. It was a wrongful course of justice, and the Finchinglakes have had to carry those rumours around with them all of their lives.'

Arthur twisted his silver moustache. 'Now, now, Hannah. Those rumours are a hundred years old, the

Finchinglakes have become renowned for their own ability since then. There was never a vineyard on the border of Truelove Hills until about fifty years ago. It was all farmland. Toby Finchinglake learnt well from his father, and it's all credit to him that the business is established enough to come into partnership with us. Theo's looked at the books, and there's no doubt we can all go into business together.'

Hannah reached into her pocket for the brooch. 'I was going to give this to Toby today, but he wasn't at the vineyard. It was found in the basement of my house.'

Arthur scrutinised the brooch and rubbed his chin. It was a long-line design, two rusty "MM's" with seven murky green stones following the letters. He handed it back to Hannah. 'The initials "MM" have intrigued me for many years. Come with me.' Arthur walked over to his writing bureau. 'I bought this for my Alice as a wedding present. I got it for a good price because there was a key missing.' Arthur pulled down the hinged writing flap to reveal several pigeon holes and small drawers. 'If you look closely at the drawer in the middle at the bottom you will see the initials "MM" in small gold lettering.'

Hannah shuddered. 'Toby Finchinglake's great-grandmother was called Mary Moon before she married into the family. There's a painting of her above the fireplace in Sophie Finchinglake's lounge. She's sitting at a writing bureau just like this, and there's an emerald box on the top. It looks like the one AJ found at Sonning Hall.'

Arthur reached on top of the bureau. 'Well, I've been a little bit naughty. When AJ told me there was a key in the emerald box, I had a look. I couldn't believe my eyes when I saw "MM" in gold writing inside the lid of it. I borrowed the key, to test if it would unlock the drawer in the bureau that Alice and I were never able to get into. It didn't matter to us at the time, just a shallow drawer that was almost hidden. There were plenty of other drawers for us to use.'

Arthur handed the key to Hannah. 'Let's see if the key opens the drawer.'

Hannah placed the key in the lock and twisted it – the drawer sprang open. Her wide eyes surveyed her grandfather, and her lawyer instinct kicked in. 'Why would the key to this bureau be in Sonning Hall?'

Arthur had the answer. 'The Finchinglakes lost everything at one point. They had some good antiques, but no cash. They started selling their best pieces and places like Sonning Hall snapped them up. All credit to them, they built the vineyard from the funds that came in.'

Arthur stared at the open bureau drawer and nodded towards it. 'Have a look through what's in there, Hannah. It must be important to lock it away and hide the key.'

Hannah's, hands trembled as she lifted out the brown envelope. It was decaying and frayed at the sides, but there was a clear stamp on the back which read: "From Mary Finchinglake (nee Moon)".

The letter was addressed to: "The owner of this bureau."

Arthur took the letter from Hannah's hands. 'We're doing nothing illegal here. I'm the owner of the bureau. Let me read the letter.'

The letter read:

To all who have ever doubted me,

My family were never dealing illegally. With emeralds, tobacco, alcohol or anything that has been linked to our name and never should have been.

The trouble was, there were too many people prepared to stand aside while my husband treated me without respect and used my dowry to fund his own means. There is only one person who tried to help me. I, thereby, leave my all to Josiah Tomlin.'

Yours truly

Mary Finchinglake (nee Moon)

'I don't know what to do, Grandpa, Toby's great-grandfather was hanged for the murder of Josiah Tomlin at Pebble Cove. I have recently seen evidence that Mary Finchinglake was involved with taking a man away from Pebble Cove at the time of Josiah Tomlin's suspected murder'.

Arthur frowned. 'Give me the letter to keep safe, Hannah, there's nothing for you to worry about. I'll sort out what needs to be done.'

Hannah hugged her Grandpa. This was all too much to take in. Maybe, after a long bath, and good sleep, things would seem different in the morning.

14

THE VINEYARD EXPERIENCE

Lady Leticia Lovett cooled her wrists under the cascading water of her replica Trevi Fountain in the courtyard of Chateau Amore de Pebblio. August was living up to its reputation of being the hottest month of the year, and the Finchinglake wines were either on ice or being kept to an acceptable room temperature before tonight's evening meal.

Leticia summoned her butler, 'Gerard! The rose petals need clearing from the terrace. Don't just throw them away, scatter them on the guest beds and make sure the towels are folded as swans.'

The bell to the entrance doors chimed, and Gerard rushed to open them. 'Good afternoon, Mr Finchinglake. We weren't expecting you so early.'

Toby smiled and clasped the butler's shoulder. 'I thought you might need some help. It's an important day, and I'd like to play my part. Show me what needs doing.'

After much persuasion, Gerard found a basket for Toby to collect the rose petals. Toby picked up the petals off the terrace and noticed several more on the grass in the Italian-styled grounds of the chateau. It felt good to be doing something worthwhile out in the open air, and he wandered around until he reached the border that backed onto Hannah's property.

A five-foot fence had been erected at the end of Hannah's garden. Toby noticed the newness of the soil and reflected on the disturbance that Lady Leticia would have had to endure over the winter months. He had admiration for both women; for Leticia's acceptance that she should sell part of her home and for Hannah's drive and determination to have the renovation work completed in record time.

Lady Leticia soon joined Toby. 'It doesn't look in keeping, does it? A brand-new fence in the chateau's grounds. It partially blocks the sea view from the terrace. I hadn't thought about that when I sold the house to Hannah.'

The Lady sighed. 'It's a shame that my husband and I weren't fortunate enough to have a family. Now that I'm on my own, the chateau is far too big. Still, I can always fill the empty rooms with guests. I'm never short of an intelligent conversation or two with visitors arriving from all over the world.'

Toby felt Leticia's loneliness as she strolled through the magnificent gardens, stopping to smell the roses on her way. He bent down and continued with his task of collecting petals. There were handfuls of pink petals beneath a bush in front of him, and he picked them up taking care not to lift any of the loose soil beneath – the Lady wanted petals, not mud. By the time Toby entered the chateau the basket was full.

Gerard was delighted. 'That is terribly kind of you, Mr Finchinglake. If you need any help tomorrow when the guests attend the vineyard, then I'm sure Lady Lovett could release me for a few hours to pop over to yours. I could drive her rather than tie up the chauffeur for the day.'

Toby's eyes twinkled. Did Gerard have a soft spot for Leticia? It wouldn't harm for the Lady to have a companion when she visited the vineyard. 'That's an excellent idea, Gerard. Having your presence there would certainly be a bonus. I'll speak to Leticia and make the arrangements. Is there a room where I could freshen up before dinner?'

Toby collected a change of clothes from his car and Gerard showed him to a spare guest room. He had an hour to get ready. As Guest of Honour and after dinner speaker he felt slightly nervous. Thirty minutes later a knock came on his door. Toby opened it to the sight of a uniformed valet holding a small silver tray. 'Letter for you, Mr Finchinglake.'

Toby lifted the white envelope off the tray and reached into his pocket for a gratuity for the valet. When the door was closed, he opened the envelope. A heavy gold ring fell into his hand, and Toby read the letter:

Dear Mr Finchinglake

You mislaid your family heirloom while collecting petals this afternoon. I found it in the basket you gave to me.

Yours sincerely

Gerard

(Lady Lovett's Butler)

Toby sat on the bed and inspected the ring. The wide gold band was studded with emeralds, and there was an engraving on the inside which read: *James Finchinglake.*

There was no denying the ring belonged to Toby's family, but he had never seen it before. How bizarre. Toby didn't have time to contemplate further, he dropped the ring into his pocket and headed down the stairs to the terrace. Pre-dinner drinks were being served, and he hoped the Finchinglake sparkling wine was being well received.

*

The following morning Lady Leticia and Gerard arrived at the vineyard ahead of their guests. Gerard inspected the tables laid in the barn ready for wine tasting.

Leticia linked arms with Toby. 'I must say your speech was excellent last night. A round of applause that lasts for over two minutes is almost unheard of.'

Toby smiled. 'I think the effect of the wine had kicked in before I finished speaking.' Leticia tutted and Toby continued, 'It's very good of you to bring Gerard along today, you should consider allowing him to accompany you on other official engagements. He'd make a good companion.'

The Lady fiddled with her three-strand pearl necklace. 'You could be right, Toby. You could be right. Oh, look, the Executive Coach is arriving now with our guests. Please excuse me.'

After a tour of the vineyard, the guests gathered in the barn to sample the different varieties of wine and enjoy a buffet lunch of locally sourced organic produce. The event was proving a huge success.

Will Tomlin felt ill at ease. 'Toby, there's

something you need to know. Hannah was here the other day, and she's intercepted some potential conflict that's coming your way.'

Toby's eyes flared. 'What do you mean by "intercepted"?'

'She's meeting a man at two o'clock this afternoon at her office in the chateau. She said it's nothing to trouble you about because she's your lawyer. I haven't got a good feeling about it though. I think she may need help.'

Toby glanced at his watch. He had fifteen minutes to get to the chateau. 'Please cover for me, Will. I'll be back as soon as I can.'

15

THE ANONYMOUS MAN

'I'm afraid I didn't catch your name when we met at the vineyard.'

'My name's Josiah Tomlin.'

Hannah twisted in her swivel chair. 'What can I do for you, Mr Tomlin?'

'I'm here to get what's rightfully mine.'

Hannah pulled the sleeve of her blouse down to cover her bracelet. 'For me to help you, I need to know what you perceive to be rightfully yours.'

'Well, this house for a start.'

Hannah's nails dug into the arms of her chair as she rose to walk towards the window of her office in

Chateau Amore de Pebblio. 'You will need to elaborate on your ancestry for me, Mr Tomlin, before I can help you.'

'My great-grandfather lived in this house before the Finchinglakes murdered him.'

Hannah paced around her office. 'It intrigues me why you do not have an accurate account of your family's past. The Tomlin's never lived in this chateau.'

The door to Hannah's office flew open, and Toby bounded in. 'Get off these premises now! I have told you before, and I will tell you again; the Finchinglakes will not be held to ransom by chancers such as you.'

The bearded man ran to the door without looking back.

'I'm sorry you had to experience that, Hannah. Unfortunately, I have to deal with idiots like him all of the time.'

Hannah gestured to Toby to sit down, and she poured him a coffee. 'Tell me all about it, Toby. Have you been threatened, blackmailed?'

'Absolutely not! I see them off before anything goes too far. The trouble is that when people dig deep into our history, they find skeletons in the closet and that makes us an easy target for low-level imposters.'

'Have you had any high-level imposters?'

Toby smiled at Hannah's concern. 'Not that I know of.'

Hannah pulled a handkerchief out of her trouser pocket and unwrapped the mouldy brooch before handing it to Toby. 'We now have potential further evidence that Mary Finchinglake visited Pebble Cove.'

Hannah sat back in her chair and peered at Toby over her coffee cup. 'Is it true that at one stage your family sold many of its assets?'

Toby's shoulders drooped, and sadness clouded his eyes. 'My grandparents had to sell everything. The rumours that surrounded us couldn't be overcome. It was my father that planted the vineyard with the proceeds of the sale.'

'Would your family's assets have gone to auction locally and been purchased by privileged houses such as Sonning Hall?'

Toby laughed. 'Sonning Hall bought a "job lot" from us. That family has always been renowned for its charitable donations. It broke my grandfather's heart to realise we had become a charity case. I've personally avoided going to Sonning Hall until recently.'

Hannah divulged her latest news. 'My grandfather has a writing bureau that belonged to your great-grandmother. A key was missing, but now we've found it. There was an envelope inside the locked drawer, supposedly written by Mary Finchinglake, leaving all of her assets to Josiah Tomlin.'

The rage that welled within Toby coloured his neck then his cheeks. 'I have never heard of such tosh! I have spent my whole life protecting my family's name, rebuilding our reputation, making the vineyard a success, giving up my chance of a relationship to protect anyone from coming into my nightmare of explaining why there are emeralds under my home. Can you give me that letter, Hannah? I need to stop all this nonsense at source.'

Hannah shook her head. 'The letter is incriminating evidence.'

'But you've given me the brooch and the photograph.'

Hannah sat down. 'I don't have time for this, Toby. You've made it clear that you don't want a relationship with me. My priority is AJ. I won't create any unnecessary distress. What happened one hundred years ago should stay there. Can we please now try to get on with our lives?'

Toby put the brooch in his pocket with James Finchinglake's ring. 'I'm sorry to have exposed you to all of this, Hannah.'

'I'll lock the letter away, Toby. There are no guarantees on my part, but things appear to have timed out. Your family lost everything after the Mary Finchinglake and Josiah Tomlin debacle, and now you have rebuilt your assets. That's all credit to you, and I wish you all the very best in dealing with your demons.'

'My demons! What do you mean by that?'

'Any excuse other than to have a meaningful relationship. I must go now, Toby, so if you could leave my office and my life, I would be extremely grateful.'

Toby slammed the office door on his way out. How could a woman treat him like that? No woman ever before had had the guts to tell him like it is was. Having said that, he'd not been interested in any woman. His priority was restoring his family name.

Looking at his watch, Toby clambered into his car. He wouldn't have time to go back to the vineyard. Will would smooth things over with Leticia and her guests. Toby's new project was about to be launched. One hour from now, Finchinglake Games Emporium was due to open.

16

FINCHINGLAKE GAMES EMPORIUM

Two weeks later Clive and Arthur reflected over their pints in the pub. They were always open to new ideas, and the new games emporium that had recently opened on the outskirts of the village sounded exciting. Arthur gave his view. 'Well, a casino in the village would be an absolute "no go", but as it's just on the edge, I think we should give it a try.'

Clive's eyes twinkled. 'Do you think they play Blackjack?' Arthur curled his silver moustache into an orderly fashion with this forefinger. 'I've always fancied a go at roulette. I must admit, I've never been to a casino, always something I wanted to do. It's on my "bucket list".'

Clive's chauffeur peered around the door of the pub. 'That's our signal, Arthur, our limousine awaits. Do you have enough cash on you? I don't know if they take credit cards in these places.'

Arthur tapped the wallet in his trouser pocket. 'I've got twenty pounds. That's my limit. If I lose it, then at least I can say I had fun trying.'

The car journey took five minutes, and Arthur and Clive stepped out of the limousine with shining eyes – their eyes were the only things shining. There was a notice on the front of a warehouse building which read: *Finchinglake Games Emporium. Under 12's welcome. After-school club. Open 4.00 pm until 6.00 pm.*

Clive gulped. 'I think we may have been a bit premature, Arthur. How fooled were we?'

Arthur managed a wry smile. Toby Finchinglake was full of surprises. Hannah knew when she was onto a good thing. 'I suggest we have a little trip back to the pub and get out the dominoes. If you've got twenty pounds, I'll match you.'

Clive shook his friend's hand. 'Done.'

*

One day later and Arthur and Clive arrived at the Games Emporium at four o'clock.

An enthusiastic doorman greeted them. 'Are you here to help with the children, or to work in the kitchen?'

Clive spoke first. 'Well, I'll give it a go working in the kitchen.'

Arthur held his shoulders back. 'I have a multitude of qualifications in looking after youngsters. Just point me in the right direction.'

The kitchen was a hive of activity, and the supervisor gave Clive the lowdown. 'When the children come here after school, they need to let off a bit of steam, that makes them hungry. We have an essential job to make sure there's enough food and that none's wasted. We're a charity you know.'

Clive put on an apron. 'Finchinglake Games Emporium is a charity?'

'Oh, yes, Mr Finchinglake wants all children to be treated equally. Some of their parents can't afford to pay for an after-school club, so we open our doors for free to any youngsters under twelve, that way no-one loses out. Mr Finchinglake raises the money to cover our costs.'

Arthur hadn't been ten pin bowling for years. He rolled a bowling ball down the middle of a lane and stood back to watch the result. 'It's called a "strike" when you get all of those pins down in one go. I got nine that time, it gets tricky now to knock down the last one, but I'll give it a go.'

Little Jimmy handed Arthur a glass of orange squash. 'I paid for that out of my own money.'

Arthur reached into his pocket for some small

change. 'Here you go, I can't have you spending your money on me.'

Jimmy held out a pot of plastic coins. 'It's all right, I've got ten pounds to spend. You helped me tie up my bowling shoes, so I wanted to buy you a drink.'

Arthur sat down and sipped the orange squash. One of the helpers sat down next to him. 'Isn't this a brilliant project? Mr Finchinglake is keen for the children to get something tangible when they spend money and not to take any risks with it. He wants them to learn the value of money at an early age. The children are given ten pounds each, in plastic money, when they arrive. They can either pay for time on a pool table, a bowling lane or any of the other activities. They need to "buy" their food and drink too. If they "save" any money then it goes into the Emporium's bank to buy new games. That way the children feel they're investing in the club.'

Jimmy was soon back at Arthur's side. 'Will you have a game of table football with me? I'll pay.'

By the time six o'clock came both Arthur and Clive were exhausted but exhilarated. Whatever the Finchinglakes had done in the past, Toby had more than restored the family's reputation. On top of his charity events, and the after-school club, he was now in partnership with Truelove Hills and the reviews for the first Vineyard Experience weekend were outstanding. There was now a waiting list for places on the joint venture. Theo, as Head of Tourism, was delighted. From the apartment above Matilda's Memorabilia, he saw Clive's limousine arrive outside the pub and wandered over to give the village's principal investor the excellent news.

Clive patted him on the back. 'That's great news, Theo! I must say I have a lot of time for Tobias Finchinglake. He's a good sort. Did you know about his after-school club?'

Theo shook his head. 'That one escaped me. How long has it been open?'

Clive chuckled. 'Oh, only a couple of weeks. Arthur and I got hold of the wrong end of the stick. We thought it was a casino!'

17

A VISIT BY JOSIAH TOMLIN

Mrs Carruthers took hold of the young man's bag. 'Let me help you into the apartment upstairs. Where have you come from?'

Josiah surveyed the interior of the Post Office & General Store. 'I am here from America. There are people I need to meet and greet.'

Mrs Carruthers narrowed her eyes. 'Why exactly are you here in Truelove Hills?'

'To discover my roots.'

Mrs Carruthers folded her arms and eyed the man up and down.

Josiah was unperturbed, and he reached for two packets of chewing gum and a newspaper. 'Put those on my bill.'

Mrs Carruthers left the shop unattended and dashed over to Arthur's cottage. 'I've got a man staying in my apartment, and I don't trust him.'

Arthur marched over the road. 'My name's Arthur Makepeace, what's yours?'

The man held out his hand to shake Arthur's. 'Josiah Tomlin. I'm very pleased to meet you, Sir, I've flown across the pond to take a look at this quaint little place. My great-grandfather came from here.'

Mrs Carruthers shuddered. She knew of the village's history – Josiah Tomlin was murdered by James Finchinglake a hundred years ago. James Finchinglake was hanged for it. She decided to keep quiet and let Arthur do the talking.

'Well, the Tomlin's had a presence in the village for many years. I was good friends with Billy Tomlin when we were boys. It's a shame that Billy's recently passed away – you could have met him. Why don't you come over to the King Arthur this evening and we can have a pint or two reminiscing about old times?'

Josiah shook Arthur's hand again. 'I'll certainly do that, Mr Makepeace, thank you for your hospitality.'

Mrs Carruthers waited for the apartment door upstairs to close before airing her concerns. 'Does he know that his great-grandfather was murdered at Pebble Cove? What's Hannah going to say if he's here to sneak around her house? He'll no doubt want to see where his family used to live. How do we know that he really is a Tomlin?'

Arthur's head was spinning as he left the shop. Instead of walking over the road to his cottage, he turned left and headed up the hill towards Hannah's house. He needed some help with piecing the Tomlin's ancestry together.

Hannah made a pot of tea and sat down with her grandfather at the kitchen table. 'What's bothering me, Hannah, is that Billy was an only child and he was born in 1932, the same year as me. He always said his father was dead. I've never put too much thought into it before; I always assumed Billy's grandfather was Josiah Tomlin, but if he was murdered in 1920 . . .'

Arthur held his head in his hands, and Hannah's heart sank. This was the last thing Toby needed, his family's past being raked up yet again, this time it may be a genuine member of the Tomlin family that had turned up. She needed to get to the bottom of Toby's angst once and for all.

'Let's make some notes, Grandpa. If we get everything down on paper then maybe we can work out the feasibility of the Tomlin's ancestry. So, Josiah Tomlin was allegedly murdered in 1920, but a body was never found. How old was he when he was last seen?'

'I don't know, Hannah. Isn't it on the internet?'

Hannah's fingers tapped away on her laptop. 'Well, it says on here that he was thirty-eight, married with no children.'

Arthur stared at Hannah. 'Who was Billy's dad then?'

The arithmetic was easy for Hannah to work out. 'Billy was born twelve years after Josiah disappeared. It appears that Billy wasn't a Tomlin after all and that his mother made up the story about his father being dead to cover up the fact that she'd had an affair out of wedlock. If she'd got married again, then Billy would have had a different surname.'

Hannah glanced sideways at her grandfather. 'We need to lock Mary Finchinglake's letter away. I'll collect it from you and keep it safe in my office at the chateau.'

'But, Hannah, what if Josiah Tomlin went to America and started a family over there? Doesn't that mean they are entitled to everything the Finchinglakes have because Mary Finchinglake wanted to give everything she owned to Josiah Tomlin? I'm not comfortable about all of this, Hannah.'

Hannah closed the lid of her laptop before taking it back into the lounge. She crossed her fingers before calling out, 'There's no concern for the Finchinglakes, Grandpa. If anything, they could sue any surviving Tomlins for the unlawful hanging of James Finchinglake.'

*

Arthur was pleased that Clive could join him in the pub that evening, he was relieved that he arrived before Josiah Tomlin.

'Hannah has her reasons to protect the Finchinglakes, as we all do, but I think she's being a bit airy fairy about dotting the "I's" and crossing the "T's". We need to put the frighteners on Josiah Tomlin so that he goes away with a flea in his ear.'

Arthur pushed Mary Finchinglake's letter across the table, and Clive read it. 'I see what you mean, Arthur. It's interesting that the lady mentioned her dowry. I'd like to look into that if I may? I have a contact who has records of such things. It may flag something up that would help us.'

Arthur nodded and retrieved the letter as Josiah walked past the pub window. He touched his finger to his nose, and Clive winked.

'Well, hello there, Mr Makepeace.'

Arthur shook Josiah's hand. 'Let me introduce you to a very important person – that's a VIP you know – his name's Lord Sonning-Smythe, and he knows the difference between right and wrong; you could say he's a kind of Judge.'

Clive choked on his beer before holding out his hand. 'Mr Tomlin, it's a pleasure to meet you. Please accept our warmest welcome to Truelove Hills.'

Arthur narrowed his eyes. 'We must say we're surprised that you're here. I take it that your great-grandfather's name was also Josiah Tomlin? What year did he turn up in America?'

'You are quite correct, Sir. All firstborn boys have taken my great-grandfather's name. Josiah Tomlin the first came to America in 1920 to make his fortune. I'm Josiah Tomlin the fourth. May I question why you're surprised I've come to visit my roots?'

'Because your great-grandfather was allegedly murdered right here on the beach at Pebble Cove and James Finchinglake was hanged because of it.'

Josiah's face turned grey. 'I don't believe it.'

Clive nodded sternly. 'I am afraid what Arthur says is true. I'll pop up to the bar and get you a pint. You look like you need one.'

Arthur leant across the table. 'The Finchinglakes

lost everything because of your family. It has taken them years to rebuild their reputation. Are the Tomlins rich in America?'

'We're one of the wealthiest families on the east coast, and the news about my great-grandfather would ruin us.'

'Well then, I suggest we draw up a compromise agreement. We'll keep your family's past a secret if you pay the Finchinglakes one million pounds for their inconvenience.'

Josiah stood up and headed for the door. 'I'm calling my attorney.' The pub door slammed just as Clive returned with the pint.

'What's up, Arthur? You've got a guilty look about you.'

'I pushed him too far, Clive. He said the Tomlin's are rich on the east coast of America, and I tried to tie him down to paying the Finchinglakes one million pounds for their inconvenience. I should have started out lower – maybe a few thousand pounds, not a million. Anyway, he's gone off to phone his attorney.'

Clive raised an eyebrow and looked at his watch. 'It's early afternoon over in America now, so his attorney will be around. Depending on how quickly Josiah Tomlin returns for his pint will give us a clue as to how his telephone call goes. Don't jump too quickly to accept an offer, Arthur. Leave the negotiating to me.'

Five minutes later the pub door opened, and Josiah returned to his seat before downing his pint. 'I must say that I feel extremely uncomfortable with all of this, I can't stay a day longer with the knowledge of my family's past hanging over me. I'll arrange for my attorney to transfer one million pounds to the Finchinglakes.'

Arthur was about to shake Josiah's hand before Clive interrupted. 'Oh no, no, no. That's not enough for the trauma that family has gone through over the last one hundred years. Let's talk in dollars – if you agree to five million, we will have the agreement drawn up and here within the hour for all parties to sign. Let's get the legalities sorted; then you can have a few more pints in the knowledge that your family has finally done the right thing.'

Josiah shook Clive's hand, and Arthur strode behind the bar to call Hannah.

Hannah's hands trembled as she typed. She made sure there was a clause in the agreement that waived any claims from the Tomlins on the Finchinglakes. Within the hour, Toby's finances would go through the roof!

*

Hannah left the pub clutching the signed contract. She caught a glimpse of her smiling face in the window of Matilda's Memorabilia and was going to have another look at her rejuvenated self in the reflection of the Post Office & General Store, but Mrs Carruthers put a stop to that.

'It has been so busy in here today, Hannah, that I didn't get chance to pop up to you with this.'

Mrs Carruthers handed Hannah another white box. Hannah jogged home and unwrapped the box. Inside it contained a red sequined cocktail dress and a note:

Dear Hannah,

You are invited to the launch of Finchinglake's latest Pinot Noir at eight o'clock tomorrow night at the vineyard. Don't be late this time, or the food will go cold.

Toby

Hannah threw the box on the sofa. That man was unbearable. How dare he tell her not to be late and choose what she should wear. The excitement of the last couple of hours was tarnished.

Matilda closed the door to AJ's room. 'Shhhhh. He's only just gone to sleep. It took three stories tonight. Did you get your urgent work sorted? What's in the box?'

Hannah lifted the box and took it into her bedroom before crossing her fingers. She bit her lip — she'd been telling far too many white lies recently, and most of them were because of that irritating Toby Finchinglake. 'Oh, nothing much, just something I ordered online. I have another favour to ask of you, Tilly, can AJ come to yours for a sleepover tomorrow night?'

'Of course, you know that Theo and I love having him, it's good practice for when little Tressler comes along. Why don't you drop him round for tea? Then you'll have time to get ready for your hot date.'

Hannah glared at her sister. 'It's not a date — it's business.'

18

AN EVENING AT THE VINEYARD

Hannah arrived at the vineyard at nine o'clock. The lucrative contract was in her briefcase on the passenger seat, and the dress was in the white box in the boot. The car park at the vineyard was empty. Hannah grabbed her briefcase and slammed the car door.

When Toby appeared around the side of the barn, his face dropped. 'You're not wearing the dress.'

'No, I'm not wearing the dress. I prefer to choose my own clothes.'

Hannah marched towards him, and when she turned the corner of the barn she stopped in her tracks. There was a lake with an island in the centre and amongst the trees on the island fairy lights and lanterns twinkled. A small table, with white tablecloth, was laid with silver cutlery, and a firepit was aglow nearby.

Toby wrung his hands together and lowered his eyes. 'I thought you'd suit red. I'm a bit under-dressed at the moment, but I've got a change of clothes in the barn for when I've done the cooking. I've kept the barbecue over here so that you don't get covered in smoke on the island.'

Hannah was speechless. She took in the full sight of Toby in his apron, his cheeks flushed with embarrassment and his eyes looking anywhere but at her. He reached over to a nearby table and poured two glasses of wine. 'Well, here it is, our latest Pinot Noir, it's not officially launched until next week, so that was a bit of a porky I told to get you here tonight.'

After half a glass of wine, Hannah's reserve was melting. 'Why did you want to get me here tonight?'

'I could say that I was sorry for being so pig-headed, or that I missed you. Which would you like me to say?'

Hannah's heart flew. 'Both will do. I have some business to discuss with you, so I had to come here anyway.'

'Shall I light the barbecue then? We can talk business over dinner. I had some news today; Clive called me. It's quite a lot to take in, and I was pleased you were coming over so that I could share it with you.'

Hannah frowned. Clive had given her the job as Toby's lawyer to advise him on yesterday's events. 'Clive made you aware of the contract with the Tomlins?'

'What contract?'

Hannah placed her glass down. 'I'll tell you later. You start cooking, and I'll pop over to the barn to get changed.'

The conversation flowed over dinner. Toby apologised for the lake being fake. His father said that the Finchinglakes had to have a lake on their property and he was determined to build one at all costs. Hannah was in hysterics when Toby advised that it was only two feet deep and that, as a boy, he always insisted on wading across to the island rather than using the elaborate bridge. Now, as an adult, he could quite see the point of not getting his feet wet.

They were toasting marshmallows on the firepit by the time the conversation stalled enough for Hannah to deliver her news. 'Something amazing happened yesterday, Toby, Josiah Tomlin's great-grandson turned up in Truelove Hills. Mary Finchinglake rescued the original Josiah Tomlin from Pebble Cove, and he went to America to start a family and establish a business that's worth millions.'

Toby raised his eyes and Hannah reached over to hold his hand. 'I don't know how they did it, but Grandpa and Clive talked Josiah into giving your family five million dollars for the inconvenience caused by the unlawful hanging of your great-grandfather. I produced the compromise agreement and inserted a clause that takes away any right of the Tomlins to make any claims on the Finchinglakes, past, present and future. So, Mary Finchinglake's letter is dead in the water, so to speak.'

Tears welled in Toby's eyes, and he leant forward to kiss Hannah softly on her lips. 'I think my news tops yours.'

'What's that?'

'Clive has advised me that Mary Moon's dowry consisted of emeralds. The emeralds in the vault under my house aren't contraband – they belonged to my family all along. Does this mean that everything's above board and my family no longer has any skeletons in the closet? Will I now be able to sleep at night?'

Hannah laughed. 'That about sums it up!'

Toby jumped up and punched the air before releasing a bellowing. 'Yeeeeesssss!!!'

Hannah smiled and clapped her hands in delight. She stood up to watch as Toby ran around the island waving his arms in the air and whooping with joy. He was out of breath as he approached her and his silver eyes shone brighter than the stars. Toby swung an arm under her legs and picked her up. 'Come with me, Hannah, we're off to find some emeralds.'

Hannah screamed as Toby waded through the lake, his designer suit soaked to the knees. She clung to his neck and hoped he wouldn't drop her but, on second thoughts, if he did, she wouldn't mind at all.

19

THE MAGIC STEPS

Toby arrived at Hannah's house at noon carrying a large bunch of flowers and a football. He'd been invited over for lunch. AJ bounded to the front door, and Hannah stood behind him to unlock it from the top.

'Hello, AJ. This is for you. I thought we could have a game of football later.'

Hannah smiled at her son. 'What do you say?'

'Thank you, Toby.'

Toby kissed Hannah on the cheek and handed her the flowers. 'It's not the time of year for yellow tulips, so I hope these will do.'

Hannah sniffed the bouquet of peach roses, cream

freesias and blue love-in-the-mist before making sense of the "yellow tulips" comment. 'It was *you* who left me yellow tulips the day we first met. How did you know they are my favourite flowers?'

'Will Tomlin thought they'd be special to you, he remembered seeing you picking yellow tulips from the garden at the Solent Sea Guest House when you were a young girl.' Toby didn't divulge that Will remembered Hannah placing a bunch on the top of her mother's coffin when the residents lined the High Street following the shocking news of Harriet's untimely death.

'Will Tomlin remembers me from back then?'

Toby winked at AJ. 'He certainly does, he says you ripped your dress playing football in the school playground. He thought you were a tomboy.'

AJ sniggered behind his hand.

'Don't you listen to him, AJ. That's not true, I ripped my cardigan and got my shoes so dirty that it took Grandpa over an hour to clean them. I had to go to bed early for a week, and Auntie Matilda brought me two biscuits every night when she came upstairs so that I didn't miss out on supper. Those were the days!'

AJ sat down on the floor of the lounge to play with his train set, and Toby joined him, while Hannah went into the kitchen to find a vase for the flowers. Wait a minute! Toby had introduced her to Will Tomlin as "Hannah Lawful", now he was saying that Will Tomlin remembered her all along. What was Toby up to? Hannah's euphoria lessened. She couldn't challenge him in front of AJ – she'd have to wait until later.

'Mummy! Can I take Toby to the beach the magic way?'

'I've told you before, AJ, it's not a magic way. It's a dirty old messy way, and I don't like you going down there on your own.'

Toby's eyes twinkled. 'What's the magic way?'

Hannah sighed. 'Grandpa paints colourful pictures sometimes. He's told AJ that the steps below the house are magic and that if you count all the way down them you can make a wish at the bottom. The only good thing about it is that AJ can now count to ninety-nine.'

Toby stood up. 'I don't believe you can count to ninety-nine, you're far too young for that. Would you like to show me how you do it?'

AJ grabbed Toby's hand and led him to the door in the floor of the kitchen. 'See you later, Mummy.'

Hannah rushed behind them and unlocked the padlock that stopped AJ from going down the steps whenever he wanted. 'Make sure you're back in an hour. Lunch will be ready by then.'

Toby sat on the floor and swung his legs into the hole, before holding out his hand to AJ. The small boy started counting on the first step and continued until he reached the bottom. 'Ninety-nine!'

Toby lifted AJ and swung him around. 'That's amazing, AJ! The steps really are magic if you can count that well at your age.'

AJ regained his balance before standing at the bottom of the steps and closing his eyes. Toby watched until AJ opened his eyes, grabbed Toby's hand and headed for the door to the beach. 'What were you doing then, AJ, with your eyes closed?'

'Making a wish. I make one every time.'

Toby pulled the door open, and the sun streamed into the basement room of Hannah's house. 'Do your wishes come true?'

'Not yet.'

Toby made a mental note to find out what AJ wished for. He'd do his best to make AJ's wishes come true.

It was ninety minutes later when Hannah struggled down the cliffside steps with a large cool bag. She stopped on one of the platforms to rest. Toby was knee-deep in the sea wading out to collect a frisbee.

Her thoughts turned back to last night. Toby certainly didn't mind getting his feet wet, a warm feeling encompassed her, quickly followed by a shudder – Toby wasn't being honest with her.

AJ ran towards his mother. 'Picnic! I'm hungry.'

Hannah placed the cool bag on the beach, and Toby looked at his watch. 'I'm sorry, Hannah, we were having such fun that I completely forgot the time. Let me help you.'

After lunch, AJ continued his search for crabs and Hannah tackled Toby. 'You've been lying to me.' Toby's pained expression cut through her. 'You told me this morning that Will Tomlin remembered me from years ago. He even told you I liked yellow tulips. You left yellow tulips at my house on the day we first met, but when you introduced me to Will, you called me "Hannah Lawful" and said that he would guess who I was if you introduced me as "Hannah Makepeace". Have you been tricking me, Toby? Was there ever an issue with your finances? Did you really need a "business consultant"?'

Toby held his hands up. 'I'm only guilty of misleading you as to when the discrepancies in my finances occurred. I'd worked out for myself that Will was syphoning off the money to pay for Billy Tomlin's funeral, and he's now paid the money back, so all of that's true. However, it all happened before my first meeting with you at the chateau. I used the quandary I'd already solved to spend time with you.'

Hannah didn't know whether to be flattered or annoyed. 'You let me believe that Sophie was your wife and sent me off on a wild goose chase investigating Will, do you realise how embarrassed I feel now?'

Toby reached for Hannah's hand. 'When I tell you the rest, you won't judge me as a stalker, will you?' Hannah narrowed her eyes and let Toby continue, 'We met two years ago in Dubai. I was there on business, and you were the lawyer in the room. I had never seen anyone so beautiful, so determined, so obnoxious, so blinkered that you didn't even notice me when I stared at you for over an hour. I asked you for a drink after the meeting, but you fobbed me off without even looking at me. When I visited your offices the following day, I left a magazine on your desk open on the page with the article and photographs of the vineyard. I thought you might pay attention to me after that, but you didn't. I had meetings in your offices for four days, but I couldn't crack through the ice to get close to the real Hannah.'

Hannah was at a loss for words, and Toby held a finger to her lips. 'I've found the real Hannah now though. It was worth the wait. Quick, AJ's not looking.' Toby leant forward and kissed her. 'Do you forgive me?' Hannah nodded and leant her head against his shoulder.

'Do you know what AJ wishes for when he counts the ninety-nine steps? I want to help out if I can.'

Hannah sat up and gazed into Toby's eyes. 'You don't have to help everyone and anyone you know. AJ's probably wishing for a new pair of trainers or a dog or something. He'll change his mind once he's got what he wants.'

Toby stood up and brushed the sand from his soggy shorts. 'I don't know, he was wishing pretty hard. I'll find out what he's after.'

AJ grinned at the sight of Toby approaching with a fishing net and a bucket. 'What do you wish for AJ? Do you wish for lots of different things? Do you wish for something new each time? Tell me your secrets. I won't tell Mummy.'

AJ looked over at Hannah then whispered in Toby's ear. 'I only ever wish for one thing.'

Toby whispered back. 'What's that?'

'A brother.'

20

FIRST DAY OF SCHOOL

September had arrived, and Sophie Finchinglake was at the school early ensuring the classroom was ready to welcome its first pupils. Today, the Alice Makepeace Academy would open its doors to seven local children.

By nine o'clock the parents and children had arrived in the playground. Hannah was there with AJ, and Toby had driven Josie and Jules from the vineyard as a favour for Sophie. It was a big day for his sister, and he knew she wanted things to be just right.

AJ pulled on his mother's arm. 'Can Josie and Jules come for tea?'

Hannah laughed. 'Of course, they can. Maybe one

day next week, when we've made lots of cakes. You'd like to do some baking wouldn't you?'

'Yeeessss, Mummy!'

Jules glanced up at Toby smiling at Hannah and whispered to AJ, 'Uncle Toby loves your Mummy.'

AJ watched as Toby placed a hand on the small of Hannah's back and leant towards her. They were both laughing. Toby had spent lots of time with them over the last few weeks, and AJ wanted the summer to go on forever. When the weather wasn't so nice, Toby wouldn't come around to play on the beach and in the garden. That made AJ sad.

Sophie opened the school doors and gestured for the children to enter. Toby hugged Josie and Jules, and Hannah kissed AJ. AJ was about to go inside when Toby called after him. 'AJ come here and give me a hug.' AJ ran to Toby and threw his arms around him. 'I didn't want to leave without saying goodbye. I have to go away for a little while, make sure you look after Mummy until I get back. We've had fun over the summer, haven't we?'

AJ nodded then turned around. Tears streamed down his cheeks as he walked into school and he wiped his eyes on his sleeve.

Sophie placed an arm around him. 'The first day of school can be a little bit scary, but we're going to be doing lots of nice things. Let me show you where you can hang your coat, and then we'll find your desk.'

The day dragged for both Hannah and AJ. When the end of school bell sounded, AJ wandered over to collect his coat, and he walked into the playground with his shoulders slumped. Hannah ran towards him. 'I've missed you so much, AJ. How was school? What did you do today?' AJ burst into tears.

Sophie wasn't far behind, and she spoke quietly to Hannah, 'I don't know what's wrong with AJ. He's been very subdued all day – it's not like him at all.'

Mrs Carruthers was waiting at the school gates. 'Here's another one of those white boxes for you, Hannah. Hello, AJ, you look glum. Why don't I come to yours for a cup of tea and you can tell me what's wrong? Tallulah's covering in the shop for the next hour.'

Hannah boiled the kettle in the kitchen, and Mrs Carruthers cuddled AJ on the sofa. 'Why are you looking so sad after your first day at school?'

Mrs Carruthers handed AJ her handkerchief, and he blew his nose. 'Have any of the children been bullies?' AJ shook his head. 'Is Sophie Finchinglake a useless teacher?' AJ shook his head vigorously. 'Well then, tell me what's up, and I'll make everything better.'

'I want my Daddy.'

'But AJ, darling, you don't have one. Your Mummy doesn't know who he is.'

'I know who he is.'

'You do! Tell me, and it'll be our secret.'

AJ shook his head, and Mrs Carruthers tried a different tactic. 'Tell me – then I can bring your Daddy back.'

AJ nuzzled into Mrs Carruthers' neck and murmured, 'Toby.'

Mrs Carruthers just knew it! All those white boxes and she'd finally succumbed to opening the one that arrived today before giving it to Hannah. 'Where's Toby gone then?'

AJ's curls swished against Mrs Carruthers' face. 'Does that mean you don't know, but that he's gone and left you both in the lurch?' AJ burst into tears again.

Mrs Carruthers was distraught. Hannah deserved better than this. She needed to let Arthur know that there was a crisis in his family. 'Don't worry about the tea, Hannah, I need to get back to the shop. See you again soon.'

Arthur pulled the door to his cottage open, and Mrs Carruthers barged in. 'I've found out who AJ's father is, it's Toby Finchinglake, and he's gone and deserted them both again.'

Arthur guided Mrs Carruthers to his window seat and put the kettle on while he digested the news. 'How did you find this out?'

'AJ told me himself. Can you believe it?'

Arthur scratched his head. Hannah had told him the other day that Toby had been to Dubai a couple of years ago and that's where they'd first met.

Mrs Carruthers enlightened Arthur further. 'Toby Finchinglake keeps sending Hannah parcels. The one today was a joy to behold.' Arthur raised his eyebrows, and Mrs Carruthers continued, 'He's proposing.'

Arthur kept his calm. Mrs Carruthers was known for spreading a rumour or two and she was full of conflicting evidence today. 'How do you know what was in today's parcel?'

'Because I opened it. I sealed it down again, of course. It was lighter than the previous ones he'd sent. It just contained a letter and a small box.'

'Did you open the letter?'

'Yes, it said something like: "Sorry to not be there on your birthday".'

'Did you open the box?'

'Of course. It contained a large murky green stone. If it was my guess, Toby Finchinglake has sent Hannah an emerald to have cut to her choice for an engagement ring.'

*

Hannah kissed AJ goodnight and opened the white box. She read the letter from Toby:

Dear Hannah

I'm sorry not to be there on your birthday next week. The box contains the first stone ever mined by Mary Moon's family. Emeralds are stones of great vision and intuition, long believed to foretell future events and reveal one's truths. I'm happy with what I've seen when I study the stone. It clarifies my mind. I hope you have the same experience.

Love Toby x

21

HANNAH'S BIRTHDAY

Hannah's birthday had arrived – along with another white box. Hannah took her time to unwrap it. She was intrigued to discover Toby's latest surprise. Hannah lifted the lid to reveal a large reel of ribbon and a letter:

Dear Hannah

Happy Birthday! If you have a clear mind and you believe it aligns with mine then tie this emerald ribbon on a branch of the oak tree at the entrance to your drive by four o'clock this afternoon.

Love Toby x

Mrs Carruthers had read the message and advised anybody and everybody that there was going to be a proposal at four o'clock that afternoon. By mid-afternoon, a crowd had gathered at the entrance to Hannah's drive.

The sound of an ice cream van startled the spectators as it sped past them. The driver parked outside Hannah's house and opened the window to offer Hannah and AJ ice creams. The blood in Hannah's veins was pumping, and her head thumped. What on earth was happening?

AJ licked his ice cream just as the sound of tyres crunched down the gravel drive towards the house. Toby emerged from his car and stared at Hannah, who raised her eyebrows and smiled. That was enough for him to know she was on the same wavelength. He fell to his knees and held out his arms for AJ to run into. 'Hold on a minute, can I have a lick of your ice cream?' AJ shoved the cornet into Toby's face, much to the amusement of Hannah.

After embracing the boy, Toby held him at arm's length. 'Look at me, AJ, I've found you a friend that you can call your brother. He really wants a brother too. Would you like to meet him?'

AJ nodded, and little Jimmy from the Games Emporium stepped out of the back of the ice cream van. Toby held both boys around their shoulders. 'This is Jimmy, and he doesn't have a brother. Will you be his brother, AJ?'

AJ looked Jimmy up and down, he was a bit taller and older he guessed, but he was smiling at AJ, and he liked the look of him. 'OK.'

AJ flung his arms around Toby's neck, and his cornet fell to the floor.

Toby lifted AJ onto his shoulders and held onto Jimmy's hand. The small group walked down the High Street to the pub for Hannah's birthday meal, waving to Mrs Carruthers and the other well-wishers as they passed.

Mrs Carruthers was beside herself. 'How can he walk down here, with the son that he abandoned for years and another one that no-one knew about?'

*

Arthur was delighted to see Jimmy. 'I'll buy *you* an orange juice this time. What are you doing here?'

'I'm AJ's new brother. Toby said AJ wished for a brother.'

Arthur narrowed his eyes and confronted Toby. 'Is Jimmy your son?'

Toby spoke in a lowered voice. 'No. He goes to the after-school club. He's a good lad, and I knew he would get on with AJ who told me he wished for a brother. I have known Jimmy all of his life. His parents have to work around the clock to support Jimmy and his sisters. It's become quite common that he spends most weekends with Sophie at the vineyard. He's grown up with Josie and Jules. Sophie's like an auntie to him.'

Matilda and Theo arrived with apologies for being late. Six months' pregnant, Matilda was glowing. 'We've had some brilliant news today; our new house will be ready in December. Cindy and Jamie insist we have the first one that's finished as they have loads of room at Sonning Hall until they find a place. I must say that living with Theo is difficult in an apartment, with a baby too it'll be a nightmare!'

Everyone raised their glasses. 'Happy Birthday, Hannah!' Hannah managed a smile. Why was Toby Finchinglake so infuriating, she had no idea what he was planning from one day to the next. Why did he say he wasn't going to be here on her birthday? Why had he turned up with a "brother" for AJ? Why had he sent her the letter about the first emerald mined by Mary Moon's family? She marched over and grabbed him by the arm.

'I am *not* on the same wavelength as you, Toby Finchinglake. What did you see when you studied the emerald that clarified your mind?'

Toby stood firm. 'Why did you tie an emerald ribbon to the oak tree?'

Mrs Carruthers rudely interrupted. 'Because she thought you were going to propose.'

Toby raised his eyebrows at Hannah. 'Is that so?'

Hannah stormed off into the back garden of the pub to the sight of tealights lining the walkways and lanterns in the trees. Toby followed her, and everyone else peered through the windows.

Toby bent down on one knee and opened a small box containing a teardrop-shaped emerald surrounded by diamonds. 'When I looked into the emerald, I could see nothing other than our future together. For me, Hannah Makepeace, there is no future without you. Will you marry me?'

The crowd in the pub couldn't hear a "yes", but they saw Toby place the ring on Hannah's finger before he embraced her. They rushed outside to join in the celebrations.

After a few pints, Arthur confided in Hannah. 'I still can't believe that Billy Tomlin was never a "Tomlin". Who got his mum pregnant?'

Hannah giggled. 'Oh, Grandpa, you are unbelievable. That happened many years ago. We need to live in the present day.'

'I'll never forget Billy Tomlin's eyes. I've never seen them on another man. Muddy brown they were.'

Hannah remembered Will Tomlin and the time she was "investigating" him. 'Well, don't you worry, Grandpa. Billy Tomlin's grandson has the same muddy brown eyes. Billy left a legacy in Will. He's the present, not the past, and he's a good man.'

Fluffy jumped up at Theo. 'What's wrong, Fluffy?' Theo turned to see Matilda perspiring profusely.

'I don't feel too good. I've come over all dizzy.'

Theo helped Matilda into his car. 'It's best we get you checked out at the hospital.'

The doctor made copious notes. 'We need to keep you in. Total bed rest for you until the baby arrives.'

Matilda's eyes bore into Theo's. 'What about my shop?'

Theo tried to contain his anguish. 'There's absolutely nothing to worry about, Tilly. Your family will help out. They always do.'

22

MATILDA'S MEMORABILIA

Hannah was the first volunteer in the shop and Toby her first customer. 'I'd like to buy one of those heart-shaped pebbles and request that your grandfather engraves it with our initials.'

Hannah smiled. 'Anything else I can do for you?'

Toby's silver eyes twinkled. 'Well, there's lots, but for now, I need you to pass this box on to the owner of the shop.'

Hannah surveyed the shoebox sized container. 'May I see what's inside?'

Toby shrugged his shoulders. 'If you must.'

Hannah lifted the lid to the sight of sparkling emeralds.

'Toby, are you sure? They must be worth a fortune?'

'I am totally sure, the craftsmanship and effort that has brought this shop to life deserve a bit of luxury. I would like to think that your grandfather could add a stone or two to his creations and maybe the paintings by the twins could depict girls with real emerald eyes; just like most of the Makepeace ladies.'

Hannah replaced the lid and pushed the box towards Toby. 'Your kindness is a fault. There is no way my family will accept a box load of emeralds. They will be insulted for not being allowed to manage their own businesses, through thick and thin. You will have to find another way to dispose of your family's fortune.'

Toby lowered his head, and Hannah shoved the box under his arm. 'Off you go now, I've got a job to do here today, and I don't need any distractions.'

Toby left, and two hours later Hannah had a customer. 'Have you any postcards of Truelove Hills?' Hannah was pleased that she knew where to find them. The customer rifled through for five minutes then turned and left the shop.

There was just one more customer before closing. 'I want a heart-shaped pebble, and I want it now. It must be engraved with the initials "CR", and I only have five minutes to wait.'

Hannah retrieved a pebble from the window display. 'These hearts are unique. They have been individually chiselled, and only my grandfather can engrave them. I can ensure your heart will be ready by tomorrow lunchtime.'

The customer sniffed and exited the shop.

Theo arrived back from the hospital. 'How's it gone today, Hannah?'

Hannah sighed. 'Only two potential customers and they left without buying anything.'

Theo's head dropped. 'I'm really worried, Hannah, I'm earning a decent wage as Head of Tourism for the village, but if the shop doesn't make a profit then our seaside home is at risk, and there's no way I can worry Tilly about this.'

*

Hannah opened a bottle of wine after AJ was in bed and lay on her sofa. Maybe there was a solution to suit all parties: Toby didn't know what to do with his emeralds, and Matilda's business was sinking. Hannah needed to swallow her pride. She reached for her phone.

'Toby, I've changed my mind. I have a better idea for the emeralds. If you loan some to my family, then we'll ensure that every purchase of twenty-five pounds and over in Matilda's Memorabilia gets a free bottle of Finchinglake wine. We'll do a promotion that runs for a month to see how it goes. Of course, you'll need to provide the wine as we will be promoting your business. We'll put a markup on all the products that contain emeralds, and give that back to you. So, all in all, it will be a win-win situation; our products will sell, and you will be reimbursed for your part.'

Toby's chest filled with pride. Hannah was proving to be the woman he knew she was. 'Deal!'

Hannah stretched out on the sofa visualising her plan. The first person she needed to speak to was her grandfather. She'd pop down to see him in the morning on her way to the shop.

*

'You're asking me to stick emeralds onto my pebbles?' Arthur was incredulous.

'Only for a few weeks until we get customers coming into Matilda's shop.'

'I thought her shop was doing well.'

'From looking at the books, she had a good start, but sales have drifted off.'

Arthur was uncomfortable. 'We'll need to make sure that Tilly knows what we're planning. How are we going to do that without upsetting her in her condition?'

Hannah frowned. 'Well, we could tell her that emeralds are stones of great vision and intuition, long believed to foretell future events and reveal one's truths.'

'What *are* you garbling on about, Hannah?'

'Trust me, Grandpa, it will bring Tilly comfort, she likes that sort of thing. Why don't you make her something special with pebbles and emeralds for her to have in hospital? It could be your first commission. Use as many pebbles as you like and go easy on the emeralds!'

Arthur rubbed his chin. He knew exactly what he would make for Tilly.

*

One week later, Arthur arrived at the hospital with the present. Tilly lifted the cloth off Arthur's basket to reveal a small pebblestone pram with emerald interior. 'Grandpa, this is amazing. I could look at it all day.'

Arthur had practised the wording: 'Don't just stare at it Tilly, read into it, emeralds are stones of great vision and intuition, long believed to foretell future events and reveal one's truths.'

Tilly held the pram to her chest. 'You sound

different, Grandpa. What you've just said you would normally describe as gobbledygook. I'm all up for my future being told, so I'll be gazing into my emeralds. Thank you so much!'

23

MUDDY EYES

Hannah had another client. Lady Leticia was undoubtedly coming up with the goods. She waited in her office at the chateau and filed her nails with ten minutes to spare. At ten o'clock, the phone rang: 'Miss Makepeace, your client is here.'

Hannah placed her nail file in a drawer and gave the all clear: 'Please send him through.'

The door to Hannah's office opened to the sight of a lady in a wheelchair being pushed by her carer. Hannah stood up and walked around her desk to make room for her visitors. 'Hello, are you comfortable sitting here? What can I do for you today?'

The lady's muddy brown eyes scanned Hannah.

'This chateau should be mine. My father had an affair with his housekeeper, my mother left him, and the chateau was sold.'

Hannah was on red alert. 'Do you have any siblings?'

The woman shook her head. 'No!'

Hannah dared to pose the question: 'If your father had an affair, then do you know if he fathered any children from the person he had an affair with?'

The woman pulled out a walking stick from the side of her wheelchair and waved it in the air. 'That makes no difference. I am the only child that lived in this chateau.'

Hannah kept her patience. 'If your father's procreation resulted in other children, they may have rights to this chateau, the same as you.'

The woman hurled her walking stick and knocked Hannah to the ground. Her carer wheeled her out to the car park to make a quick exit. Two hours later, Lady Leticia noticed the door to Hannah's office ajar. 'Help me, someone please help me.'

Leticia rushed past the desk to see Hannah lying on the floor. 'Oh, my dear Lord, what has happened to you? We need to get you to the hospital.'

Hannah couldn't speak; she was in total shock.

From passing out to regaining consciousness, she daren't move. The trickle of thick warm blood down the side of her face when she lifted her head made her rigid. It had been best to press her forehead to the floor and wait for help.

Matilda was Hannah's first visitor. 'Look at you! That's quite a black eye. They say you took a bump to the head. Who would ever have imagined, a couple of weeks ago, that we'd both end up in hospital at the same time? What on earth happened to you?'

Hannah's head thumped, and she touched the bandage wrapped around her forehead. 'I had a fight with an old lady and came off worse. I must look a right state.'

*

Toby helped Hannah out of his car. 'Are you sure you want to stay here alone with AJ? You can both come to the vineyard with me.'

Hannah was insistent. 'I'm fine, Toby. Stop fussing. The only thing I need you to do is to ask Lady Leticia to visit me as soon as possible.'

*

Leticia sat on Hannah's sofa with her hands in her lap. 'So, are you telling me that there could be a claim on the chateau? That it should have been kept in the family and that a previous Lord couldn't keep his trousers up when the housekeeper was around?'

Hannah smiled. 'I'm saying nothing of the sort. I'm sure your husband arranged for the contracts to be drawn up to protect you from any eventualities. I just wanted you to be made aware of the "Tomlin" connection so that you can avoid any unnecessary worry if anyone turns up telling you they are entitled to things.'

'Is there a serious risk of that?'

'No, I don't believe so. The only surviving Tomlin in the UK is Will Tomlin; he's Toby Finchinglake's accountant. He has the same muddy eyes as the old woman who claimed to be the only child of the previous owner of the chateau. My grandfather reliably informs me that Will's grandfather, Billy Tomlin, the former housekeeper's son, had the same unusual eyes. From evidence that has recently come to light in relation to the Tomlin's ancestry, there is a very good chance that Billy Tomlin was fathered by the previous Lord of the chateau, meaning that Will Tomlin is a direct descendant.'

Leticia stared at Hannah. 'What if the old woman turns up again?'

Hannah's eyes narrowed. 'I doubt we'll see her again, but if she chooses to show her face then let me know, and I will sue her for grievous bodily harm.'

Leticia let out a sigh of relief. 'I'm intrigued by your reference to muddy eyes. I've never thought of them that way before.'

Hannah stared at the Lady out of her one good eye. 'Please enlighten me, Leticia.'

'There's a portrait in one of the hallways at the chateau of a Lord with "muddy-looking" eyes. I was surprised that the previous owners left it. Do you think I should offer it to Will Tomlin?'

Hannah's head hurt. 'Will's a nice young man. He's not aware of the potential scandal we've uncovered regarding his ancestry. Toby tells me he lost his father years ago and he's only recently buried his grandfather. This is something we need to leave alone.'

*

Leticia returned to her chateau and picked up the telephone. 'Tobias, it's Leticia. I require a reliable accountant. Do you know of one? What's that? Will Tomlin? Yes, that would be acceptable. Please send him over in the morning.'

The Lady ended the call. Maybe she didn't need to be alone for the rest of her life. She could take Will Tomlin under her wing and, when the time came, he could rightfully become the heir to his family's fortune

– the family he never knew existed.

24

EMERALDS FORETELL THE FUTURE AND REVEAL ONE'S TRUTHS

Matilda had been in hospital for two months and was becoming restless. Part of her daily routine was to spend at least half an hour staring into the emerald pram. She could imagine all sorts of things when she watched the darting shards of green light bounce off the walls of her room. She was becoming quite a fortune teller to her sisters, who laughed at her seriousness when she gave them exciting news about their futures. Maybe she could tell fortunes in her shop after she'd had the baby? Whatever way, she'd been advised by Theo that her business was booming since Toby Finchinglake had provided the emeralds and wine.

The sun streaming through the window was bright for the 5th of November and Matilda climbed out of bed to place the pram on a windowsill where it would best catch the light. At eight months' pregnant Matilda felt tired most of the time. She climbed back into bed and closed her eyes; the dream that encompassed her was like watching a movie.

An extended Makepeace family were on a beach. There were lots of children. A little girl in a pink dress was sitting on Matilda's lap blowing bubbles. Matilda was enjoying the scene until the dream turned to black and white and switched to the garden of the chateau. A woman in a long cloak was pushing something into a hole.

Matilda screamed, and a midwife ran into the room. Fluid was dripping from the bed onto the floor. 'There's nothing to worry about, Matilda. Your waters have broken, that's all. It's a little bit early for baby Tressler, but he's a good size. He'll be coming to meet his Mummy today.'

Matilda tried to sit up in bed, but the pain shot right through her. The midwife reached for gas and air and pressed the emergency button. 'Can someone phone Mr Tressler? Baby is on his way.'

Matilda screamed again, and managed to blurt out: 'It's a girl, I know it's a girl.'

*

Two hours later, Matilda and Theo cradled baby

Mollie. Theo stroked his daughter's wispy hair and squeezed Tilly's hand. 'She's got your blue eyes.'

Matilda smiled at the midwife. 'When can we go home?'

'The doctor will let you know. Mollie's a little bit early, but a good weight at nearly six pounds.'

*

It was champagne all round in the King Arthur. Tallulah was ecstatic. 'Perfect timing by my niece. There'll be fireworks on her birthday every year!'

Hannah, Toby and AJ took balloons and flowers to the hospital. Hannah's eyes welled up when she held Mollie. 'She's so tiny. Welcome to the world, little Mollie.'

AJ stared at the baby. 'Can I have a sister?'

Theo laughed and winked at Toby. 'Toby picked AJ up. Maybe one day.'

Hannah raised her eyes. 'Do I get a say in any of this?'

At the pub, Tabitha grabbed Rob's hand. 'Can you drive me into town? We need to get some decorations for tonight. We can turn it into a real party!'

Arthur whistled as he sat in his armchair and

polished his shoes. The writing bureau caught his eye – the secret drawer wasn't shutting properly now. He put down his shoes to examine it. There was an envelope caught at the back. The words on the front read: "*My Confession*".

Arthur took a sip of tea and reached for his letter opener. The letter wasn't addressed to anyone in particular, so it was a case of "Finders Keepers". Arthur sat back down in his chair with the letter and his mug. Struggling to hold onto both he sloshed tea all over the letter and his trousers.

'Oh, botherations! I'll need to get changed now before the big party.' Arthur placed the half-empty mug and the letter on the draining board in the kitchen.

The door to Arthur's cottage flew open. 'Grandpa, it's Tallulah, I've brought Fluffy back from his walk.' Fluffy sniffed the drips of tea on his way into the kitchen and barked when he reached the sink. Tallulah followed him. 'What's up, Fluffy?'

Arthur came out of his bedroom and picked up the letter. The faded words were even harder for him to read now that they'd been doused in tea. Tallulah could see her Grandpa struggling with his eyes. 'Let me read that for you, Grandpa.'

Tallulah tried to decipher the writing, and she read the letter slowly:

To whoever reads this,

Before I go to my grave, I need to confess that I murdered my husband and buried him on the cliff above Pebble Cove. My good friend Josiah Tomlin never knew. I paid the hangmen with emeralds for their silence. James Finchinglake did not go to the gallows – I murdered him first.

Please, God, forgive me. May I now rest in peace.

Yours truly,

Mary Finchinglake (nee Moon)

Tallulah laughed. 'What a load of old tosh! Just another one of Matilda's exaggerated stories. Her imagination is out of this world. Luckily, you've only ruined one of her "masterpieces". Let's throw it away before you get in trouble for slopping your tea. I won't tell her if you don't.' Tallulah winked at her Grandfather, screwed the soggy letter up and shoved it in the bin.

Arthur winked back. All that happened a hundred years ago needed to stay there.

*

AJ wore ear defenders in the garden of the pub while David Makepeace set off the fireworks from the field at the back near Arthur's shed. The telephone rang behind the bar in the pub and Tallulah answered it. 'It's me, Tilly, I'm lying here in hospital with Mollie thinking about you all tonight. Theo's just left. He's on his way to the pub now.'

'Tilly! I'm the proudest auntie ever! I'm struggling to hear you over all the bangs outside. AJ's loving every minute of it. That's a turn up for the books with Mollie arriving so early. Talking of books, how's your latest one coming along? Don't go incriminating the Finchinglakes whatever you do. They're part of our family now! Love you, Tilly, sleep well. I'll be in to see you if you don't get home in the next couple of days. Must go now, the Copperfield brothers are drinking outside with the regulars. They've really left me in the lurch behind the bar. Tabitha's no better. She's still making puppy eyes at Rob Sharnbrook. Love you lots, Tilly, give Mollie a big hug from me. Speak soon.'

Matilda cradled her daughter. Today had been the best day of her life. How spooky that she'd dreamed of having a little girl this morning? She reached for the emerald pram and showed it to Mollie. 'This is special, Mollie, it let me know that I was having you.'

*

When Arthur got home, he put his bin out for the next morning's collection. He went to bed and couldn't sleep. He got dressed and staggered out of his kitchen door with a torch, through the garden and over to his shed. He'd kept a bag of bones in there that Fluffy had unearthed during Hannah's building work in the chateau's grounds. His conscience had been pricking ever since. He was certain they weren't bones of deceased pets; they were too big – they were human bones.

Arthur picked up the bag and threw it in his bin. If Mary Finchinglake wanted to die with a clear conscience then so did he. There was nothing to be gained by dredging up the past.

25

SEA VIEW VILLAS

It was the 10th of December, and the first seaside house was ready. Clive proudly presented the keys to Matilda and Theo in front of a group of onlookers that had congregated down the new road that led to the beach. 'It gives me great pleasure to present you with the keys to your new home, may you all be very happy in Sea View Villas.'

Cindy, Jamie and Sebastian were there to witness their future neighbours' delight. Jamie slapped Theo on the back. 'Ours will be ready in February. We can't wait to move in. I wonder who will buy the others?'

Theo grinned at his best friend. 'Who knows, we'll have to wait and see. It'll be a big change for all of us.'

Jamie stood with hands on hips surveying the

view. 'I can't wait for us to bring our families up down here, what better place than at the seaside. What's this I hear about you buying a boat?'

Theo glanced at Tallulah. 'Well, I did kind of promise Tallulah that we could take all the provisions by boat from here to Pebble Cove when Hannah has one of her get-togethers, it's a bit of a struggle carrying everything down the cliff.'

'That was very gallant of you, Theo, I hope it's a speed boat.'

Theo looked Jamie straight in the eyes. 'With the Makepeace family? It'll need to be a ferry!'

The friends chuckled, and Cindy wandered over. 'What's so funny, you two? I can't wait to get back to Truelove Hills or to work. Profits aren't great at the bakery, delicatessen or bistro. It's not good when I can't be around to keep an eye on things. Bruce and Steve spend all their time working in the pub and, as you know, I'm relying on local staff to run things.'

Matilda joined the threesome. 'It's a worry when you have to leave your own business in the hands of others. I can't keep relying on my family for much longer to help out at my shop. They've been brilliant, but in the New Year I'll have to advertise for help.'

Jamie rubbed his hands together. 'I'm sure you'll get lots of takers with all those emeralds you're selling and bottles of wine you're giving away. Your new staff will be dripping in jewellery and drunk!'

Matilda's face clouded over. 'Don't worry me.'

Jamie waved his hands in the air. 'I'm only joking!'

Tallulah nudged Matilda. 'Well, are you going to go inside and give us the grand tour? I'm due back at the pub in fifteen minutes.'

Theo picked Tilly up. 'I didn't do a brilliant proposal, but at least I can carry you over the threshold of our new home.'

*

Clive and Arthur put on the hard hats and Hi-Vis vests provided by Rob Sharnbrook. 'Come with me, and I'll show you around the other four properties. Jamie and Cindy are buying the one next door to Matilda and Theo. It will be finished in eight weeks, weather permitting.'

Arthur was impressed. 'You'd never have guessed that these old buildings would scrub up so well. They're all so different. You've hit on a winner here, Clive.'

Clive's turquoise eyes twinkled. 'I'm considering keeping ownership of the final three villas and letting them out as short-term rentals. I've become quite fond of them. That way, I can have a say in the interior designs and name them as I wish.'

Arthur was intrigued to know the thinking behind Clive's decision. What was his friend up to? Surely selling the villas would be the best option. Clive had lots of projects on the go, and the villas would quickly sell to release immediate cash. Arthur wanted to get to the bottom of Clive's change of heart.

'What would you name the villas if you kept them?'

'Oh, that's easy: Villa Julianna, Villa Elena and lastly, but not least, Villa Veronique.'

It was the turn of Arthur's eyes to twinkle. 'You old devil. You're naming them after your girlfriends.'

Clive's wistful expression confirmed Arthur's suspicion. 'Not my girlfriends anymore, Arthur. They're the ones that got away.'

*

With David Makepeace giving Bruce and Steve Copperfield the day off from the pub to help with removals, the furniture in Matilda and Theo's apartment was soon transferred to their new home by the sea.

Mrs Carruthers left it an acceptable amount of time for the family to settle in before her first visit – she closed the Post Office & General Store early and knocked on their door at four o'clock.

Theo showed her into the lounge. 'Well, this is very spacious. You could do with some more furniture. I might have some bits I could give you. Where's Matilda?'

Theo cringed at the thought of Mrs Carruthers' offer. 'That's very kind of you, but we like to keep things simple. Mollie will be crawling soon so the less furniture, the better. She'll have more space to move around.'

Mrs Carruthers laughed. 'You're so funny, Theo Tressler. Mollie's only five weeks' old. I know some new fathers think their babies are advanced, but that's pushing it a bit.'

Matilda sniggered from the landing. 'Come upstairs, Mrs Carruthers. You can be the first person to see Mollie's nursery.'

Mrs Carruthers sat down in the white rocking chair with pink polka dot cushion. 'Whoever would have thought it, that Matilda Makepeace would do so well for herself. I'd like to take some of the credit; it was me who put a roof over Theo's head when he first came here.'

Matilda smiled, and Mollie stretched in her Moses basket. 'We would never have managed without you, Mrs Carruthers.'

Theo was worried about what Mrs Carruthers was planning for their three spare bedrooms. They only contained packing boxes. Furniture for them would have to wait for the time being. He called up the stairs, 'I've put the kettle on, at least we can offer you a cup of tea before you leave.'

Two cups of tea and a packet of chocolate biscuits later, Mrs Carruthers delved into her bag. 'I nearly forgot; I've bought you a house warming present.'

Matilda unwrapped the small package to reveal a walnut.

Mrs Carruthers nodded towards it. 'Go on, open it. My father made it for me when I was a girl.'

Matilda carefully prised the walnut apart to reveal a miniature china baby wrapped in a blanket. 'This is so unusual. It must be very sentimental to you. We can't possibly keep it.'

Mrs Carruthers wouldn't take "no" for an answer. 'I don't have many family heirlooms, but the ones that I do need to go to good homes. Having a clear out now and again is good for the soul.'

Matilda and Theo waved from the front door, and Mrs Carruthers turned around several times to wave back. Matilda was the first to speak. 'You don't think she's planning on retiring, do you?'

Theo shook his head. 'Mrs Carruthers? No, never.'

26

CHRISTMAS EVE

Two weeks later, a Christmas tree stood proudly in the window of Villa Tressler. 'Happy Anniversary, Tilly! Where has the last year gone?'

Tilly carried Mollie down the stairs and joined Theo to look through their lounge window at the sea. 'I can't believe how lucky we've been, Theo. If you hadn't chased after me, I'd still be in New York, and you'd be working in London.'

Theo raised an eyebrow. 'Is that so? If my memory serves me right, it was *you* who chased after *me* in the first place.'

The sound of the telephone interrupted their banter. 'Jamie! I know. Tilly and I were just saying the same thing. We can't believe we've all been married a year. Happy Anniversary to you and Cindy too! Just a point to mention, Jamie, you will need to think of a name for your villa, there are no house numbers down here. We've gone for the easy option of Villa Tressler for ours. I can't believe you'll be living next door to us in six weeks! See you later for carols outside the pub. Mrs Carruthers has arranged for the Salvation Army to come along. I suggest we get there early or there'll be no mince pies left, Tilly's put brandy in them.'

*

Jamie joined his father in the drawing room at Sonning Hall, the fire was roaring, and Cindy had just taken Sebastian upstairs for his nap. 'We need to name our villa. Any ideas? Theo and Tilly are calling theirs "Villa Tressler". That works well. "Villa Sonning-Smythe" would be a bit of a mouthful, though.'

Clive placed the book he was reading on an occasional table and stood with his back to the fire. 'I think you should name it from your heart. What's special to you?'

Jamie gripped his dark blonde hair in both hands and closed his eyes. 'I've got it! I just need Cindy's approval.'

Jamie dashed up the stairs to the nursery just as Cindy shut the door behind her with a finger to her lips. Jamie grabbed her hand and pulled her into their bedroom. 'Do you remember how we first met?'

Cindy laughed. 'I certainly do; it was a disaster. I was looking forward to that picnic in the Summer Hut until Mrs Carruthers interfered.'

Jamie's eyes widened. 'Do you remember when we cheated with the compatibility questionnaires that Papa and Lady Leticia produced?'

Cindy's blue eyes sparkled. 'I remember rolling around on the bed in the Summer Hut in fits of giggles at the questions they came up with.'

Jamie held both of Cindy's hands in his. 'We had fun up at Pebble Peak in the Glamping huts, didn't we?'

Cindy nodded, and Jamie continued, 'We need to name our new home and, with your approval, I think we should call it "Villa Summer".'

Tears rolled down Cindy's cheeks. 'That's perfect, just perfect, Jamie.'

Jamie handed Cindy his handkerchief. 'Dry your eyes. There's no time for tears; your parents will be here in half an hour. At least the weather's kinder this year than last with no flights cancelled.'

Cindy threw her arms around Jamie's waist. 'I loved our white wedding.'

TRUELOVE HILLS – MYSTERY AT PEBBLE COVE

Jamie stroked his wife's long blonde hair, how lucky was he? He'd married the girl of his dreams; he had an adorable six-month-old son, and in six weeks they would be moving into Villa Summer.

The hum of machinery started up outside, and huge blasts of snow shot past the window. Jamie and Cindy burst into fits of giggles. Trust Clive. He'd got the snow machines out again. Little Sebastian's first Christmas would be well and truly white.

Cindy knelt on the window seat. 'You don't think that Arthur's going to turn up later dressed as Father Christmas again, do you?'

Jamie smiled. 'There's no need. It's Christmas Eve. The real Father Christmas is already on his way.'

*

Arthur sat in his chair in the window of his cottage and gave Fluffy a piece of his biscuit. 'All's well that ends well, Fluffy. What a year! Everything's in order now, though. It's good to have a bit of a rest. We should both have a nap before we go to the carol singing later. I've bought you a new collar to wear as a Christmas present. Ruby red's a good colour for Christmas, so's emerald green.'

Arthur took a sip of tea and another bite of biscuit. He glanced over at the ruby red collar on top of his writing bureau; he was pleased he'd bought the red one for Fluffy. 'Now we need to have a discussion about digging up bones. If you find any bones in future, you should leave them where they are, or you will get me into all sorts of trouble.'

The fire was glowing in the hearth, and Arthur was at peace. Within five minutes, he was snoring. Fluffy cuddled up to his master, and seconds later he was lost in slumber too. The firelight reflected on the secret drawer in the bureau. The two gold "M's" shone brightly for over an hour before dulling as the fire went out. Nothing lasts forever; even secrets and lies can become buried in the distant past.

*

At the vineyard, the barn was a hive of activity. A giant Christmas tree stood in the centre, and Sophie was dressed as an elf. AJ, Jimmy, Josie and Jules were covered in glitter, glue and cotton wool and all painstakingly helping to make "Finchy the Formidable Snowman" out of old wine barrels.

With AJ engrossed in the snowman task, Toby and Hannah decided to take a stroll around the vast grounds of the vineyard. Toby had been contemplating his next project, and he felt the time was right to mention it to Hannah. 'Truelove Hills needs a nursery. I'd like to fund the development of one. You never know, we might need to use it one day. What should we call it?'

Hannah frowned. She wasn't usually creative, but Toby brought out a relaxed side of her that she never knew existed. Her cheeks were already pink from the cold, so she dared to risk any embarrassment by divulging a name that just sprang to mind from nowhere. 'How about "Little Finchies & Friends".'

Toby placed his arm around Hannah's shoulders. 'That's brilliant! I'll source a suitable property early in the new year.'

Toby held Hannah's hand as he pulled her up a hill on the edge of the estate. 'Are you sure you're happy about moving to the vineyard?'

Hannah's feet were freezing and she wondered how far up the hill they were going to climb. Her breath was clearly visible in the cold afternoon air, but there was no hesitation in her voice. 'I'm absolutely certain. The vineyard needs me.'

Toby raised an eyebrow and looked down at her. 'Why does the vineyard need you?'

'Because AJ can play with Jimmy when he comes to visit.'

'OK. That's a good reason. Give me another one.'

'So that you have help with renovating your family home in the utmost taste.'

'I'll give you that!'

'Also, don't forget I need to be here to keep an eye on Will Tomlin.'

They'd reached the top of the hill and Toby pulled Hannah into him to survey the vineyard below. He rubbed her gloved hands in his. 'That's an old requirement. Between you and me I think Lady Leticia will buy your house back and give it to Will. She can knock down the fence and treat him as part of her family.'

It was Hannah's turn to raise her eyebrows. 'That would work out well.'

'Now, Hannah Makepeace, give me the real reason you want to move to Finchinglake Vineyard.'

'So that AJ can walk through the lake to the island in the middle – on warmer days of course.'

Toby's eyes glistened. 'I love you, Hannah Makepeace.'

Hannah's cheeks glowed. 'I love you more, Mr Finchinglake.'

EPILOGUE

Six Months Later

Lady Leticia sat on the terrace of Chateau Amore de Pebblio and poured a glass of lemonade for Will Tomlin. 'There really is no reason to pay me rent for the house. If you help out with my accounts and join me for dinner on the odd occasion that will suffice. What do you normally do at Easter and Christmas? Do you have any family nearby?'

Will lowered his head. 'I always visited my grandfather on such occasions. We used to have a whale of a time, just the two of us.'

Leticia felt embarrassed to have been so insensitive. 'Well, I insist that from now on you join me at the chateau. Oh, look over there! They're taking the fence down. You don't need a postage stamp of a garden when the chateau's grounds are at your disposal.'

Will stood up and shielded his eyes from the sun.

'That's a big improvement already. It's very kind of you to give me access to the chateau's grounds. The last thing I would want, after a week at work, is to spend the weekend doing gardening.'

*

At the vineyard, Hannah had invited her family around for afternoon tea on the island in the middle of the lake. AJ and Jimmy sat on the edge of the lake with the fishing nets and buckets Arthur had retrieved from the basement of Hannah's house. He'd bought some plastic fish and crabs and thrown them into the lake for the boys to "catch".

Toby handed Arthur a beer, and the sun bounced off the emerald-studded ring on his finger. Arthur hadn't noticed Toby wear it before. 'New ring?'

Toby took it off and handed it to Arthur. He sat down next to him with a glass of wine. 'It's quite remarkable really, but I helped out in the garden of the chateau – picking up rose petals would you believe. Somehow my great-grandfather's ring turned up in the flower beds. He must have dropped it in the chateau's grounds over a hundred years ago. Look inside the band; it's engraved with his name.'

The ring burned Arthur's hand and he handed it back to Toby. 'Well, what a co-incidence that is. Amazing, truly amazing.'

TRUELOVE HILLS – MYSTERY AT PEBBLE COVE

*

At the chateau, the builders had taken down the fence panels and were now pulling out the concrete posts. Rob Sharnbrook sighed at the sight of more bones. He could only guess that the previous owners had buried all their pets down this end of the garden. In the olden days, they'd have had horses too, some of the bones were too big for a dog or a cat. He bagged the bones up with the rubble and threw them into a skip.

*

One hundred years on and all evidence of the crime had been destroyed – Mary Finchinglake had accomplished the perfect murder.

****

Now available in the Truelove Hills series!

TRUELOVE HILLS

The Matchmaker

Secrets and lies in Truelove Hills can lead to only one thing - a weekend that changes everything . . .

Twins, Tabitha and Tallulah Makepeace, are inseparable. They've grown up in Truelove Hills; work in their father's public house and even live above it. The only time they've been away from home was when they went to art school in London – which, of course, they went to together. Now at twenty-three years' old, their lives could be considered boring. Romance is considerably lacking; working behind the bar with Steve and Bruce Copperfield is a chore. Bruce still holds a light for Tallulah after a brief fling months ago, and Tabitha put a stop to Steve's advances before they even got off the ground.

However, there's help on the way; Lady Leticia Lovett is keen to see the two youngest Makepeace girls settle down like their elder sisters, Hannah and Matilda. The new nursery manager, Miss Mae, also wants to lend a helping hand. Between them, Lady Lovett and Miss Mae organise a Matchmaking event at Chateau Amore de Pebblio for the August Bank Holiday weekend. Tallulah is reluctant to attend, but Tabitha is willing to give it a go. Little do they know it will be a weekend that will change their lives forever.

Printed in Great Britain
by Amazon